an insiders novel

break every rule

Also in this series:

the insiders
pass it on
take it off

break
every rule

an insiders novel

by j. minter

BLOOMSBURY

BLOOMSBURY

Published by Bloomsbury Publishing, New York, London, and Berlin
Distributed to the trade by Holtzbrinck Publishers

Library of Congress Cataloging-in-Publication Data
Minter, J.
Break every rule : an insiders novel / J. Minter.—1st U.S. ed.
p. cm.
Summary: The friendship of five wealthy Manhattan teens is threatened by a contest to choose the Hottest Private School Boy.
ISBN-10: 1-58234-667-4 ● ISBN-13: 978-1-58234-667-0 (pbk.)
[1. Friendship—Fiction. 2. Dating (Social customs)—Fiction. 3. New York (N.Y.)—Fiction.] I. Title.
PZ7.S3872Br 2005   [Fic]—dc22   2005012233

ALLOYENTERTAINMENT   Produced by Alloy Entertainment
151 West 26th Street
New York, NY 10001

First U.S. Edition 2005
Typeset by Hewer Text Ltd, Edinburgh
Printed in the U.S.A.
10 9 8 7 6 5 4 3 2 1

Bloomsbury Publishing, Children's Books, U.S.A.
175 Fifth Avenue, New York, NY 10010

All papers used by Bloomsbury Publishing are natural, recyclable products made from wood grown in well-managed forests. The manufacturing processes conform to the environmental regulations of the country of origin.

for TMB

"Flan and Jonathan, sitting in a tree, K-I-S-S-I-N-G. First comes love, then comes . . ."

You know the rest.

That's what my stepbrother, Rob, singsonged when he walked in on me and Flan making out in the bathroom. I didn't know that people in Spain learned the exact same songs in second grade. How educational.

Flan was sitting on the sink with her left leg draped around my waist, and I was standing in front of her with my hands at the small of her back. We'd been getting ready to go out, and we'd had a little fight, and we'd made up. We were make-up fooling around, and it was tender and hot in that particular, forgiving way.

You're probably wondering how this romantic moment got interrupted by my eurotrash stepbrother, who should have been at least an ocean away but now wouldn't leave the bathroom. To answer that, we're going to have to back up a little bit, to . . .

Last Winter: That's when my dad married a woman named Penelope Isquierdo Santana Suttwilley, who had a son, just my age, named Rob. We met on Dad's honeymoon, which was also when I realized that my new stepbrother was annoying and prone to fashion disasters. Then my mom—acting very "I'm bigger than all of this"—said Rob could stay in our apartment, in my older brother Ted's room.

Ted's room and my room have an adjoining bathroom.

Then, post-Honeymoon: I went on this educational cruise through the Mediterranean with the guys I've been friends with since fifth grade—Arno, Mickey, Patch, David and me, Jonathan. (Sometimes people call us the Insiders, although none of us ever would.) And while we were getting lost and mad at each other over there, Rob was worming his way into my life back in Manhattan. See, David got kicked off the boat, and when he got shipped back home, all of us pretty much ignored him. Not on purpose, but Arno and Mickey were sparring over this girl named Suki, and then they were sparring over this girl named Greta. And

2

then Patch started going out with Greta, and I kind of made out with Suki. Anyway . . . all of that is pretty much forgotten.

Except the part about David. That's when he started spending a lot of time with Rob, and the friendship stuck. I think he might have that illness where you start to love your captors—Stockholm Syndrome, or whatever that's called. Rob started going out with Patch's older sister, February, and David spent some time with Patch's little sister, Flan—my Flan—thinking he might maybe have a crush on her. And so you can see how things have gotten a little bit complicated.

So, Back In New York: There's been some splintering of my crew. This is mostly on me. I'm usually the one who keeps us all together and hanging out, but since I started going out with Flan for real, I haven't been playing that role so well. And I feel bad about that, but what can you do? If David's still pissed about not getting enough e-mails while he was home alone, and the fact that Flan chose me, it's not my fault. He's not helping matters any by pretending he's something he's not, either.

See, David and Rob started spending a lot of time with Arno, and now they're like a mini side clique. They're all rocking the same hair, too: a sort of mod style with their bangs in their eyes. They look like the wannabe Beatles, minus a drummer.

Which brings us to tonight: Thursday, opening night of the big Luc Vogel retrospective at the Museum of Modern Art, and everyone's going to be there.

I told Flan to be at my house at six-thirty, but she showed up at quarter of eight. That turned out to be perfect timing, though, because I'd just finished putting on my new Duncan Quinn suit and was checking it out in the bathroom mirror. I needed a second opinion because it was British khaki, and I wasn't sure how the color was going to go over. When she walked through the door I popped my collar and said, "Hey gorgeous. How do I look?"

She sat down on the edge of the tub and crossed her legs.

"You look good," she said, smiling sort of faintly at me. "The Duncan Quinn really suits you." Then she took one of the magazines out of the magazine rack, and started looking over it like she was bored.

The last couple of weeks have been like this: full of the exquisite agony of a thousand little fights and misunderstandings, the kind that get forgotten quickly with a lot of making out. It was the beginning of spring, and all the white buds were opening on the trees. All the girls were out in their new dresses, and showing off the tans they got during winter weekend getaways to St. Bart's. After months of winter, it seemed like everything was new and warm, and everybody was in love. Or maybe that was just us. Flan and I just had our three-month anniversary.

I bent over and kissed her on the cheek. She was wearing a pink Zac Posen cocktail dress—which her older sister, February, got to keep after she modeled it in his spring fashion show last winter—and white Marc Jacobs cowboy boots. She smelled all roselike and clean, and her hair was perfectly brushed, almost like no two strands were overlapping, and pulled into a low ponytail.

"What's the matter?" I asked.

"Nothing," she said, turning a page. "It just seems like sometimes you are, like, obsessed."

I pushed the hair back from her ear, and kissed it softly. "Hey, you look beautiful. If sometimes I don't tell you that right away, it's because it's so obvious to me, and it would be, you know, redundant to say it again."

She tossed the magazine over her head and smiled wide. "Okay, you're forgiven. Now kiss me for real," she said, and put her long, slender arms around my neck.

I lifted her up and put her on the sink, and we started kissing.

That brings us to Right Now: Rob just walked into the bathroom, where he stayed, clapping and whistling, for way longer than was necessary.

"Flan," he said, "you are *del fuego* in that dress!"

"Rob, what are you doing in here?" I was irritated, and I tried to let it show.

"Can I use your Sebastian hair mold?" Rob said, brushing past us toward the mirror. I had to move fast and lift Flan out of his way. I sat down on the edge of the tub, and Flan sat on my lap. We stared at Rob in disbelief. He was looking at himself intently in the mirror, making virtually imperceptible changes to his carefully messed-up hair. Then he moved on to untucking his floral, button-down shirt ever so slightly from one side of his leather pants.

"So this night, it's going to be wild, no?" he said, still without looking at us. "I've never even been to the MAMI," he added. Rob is part Venezuelan, part French, entirely international party boy, and not exactly the best speaker of English. Flan and I tried to stifle our laughter.

"I believe the correct pronunciation is *MoMA*," I said.

"Whatever," he said. "I'm audi. The Wildenburgers invited me to a cocktail party at their house before the MAMI thing. All the famous artists to be there. I'm sure Arno would have invited you, but he only was allowed two of his friends, and that was David and moi. Ciao."

And that's when my stepbrother, thankfully, left the bathroom.

"I can't believe your sister went out with that eurotrash loser," I said.

"Yeah, neither can she," Flan giggled.

I was quiet for a minute, and then Flan snuggled into my neck and said, "Hey, are you okay? You didn't want to go to that party at the Wildenburgers', did you?"

"Nah," I said. "It's going to be all boring old art collectors and smelly cheeses."

Flan stood up and started brushing the wrinkles out of her dress. I stood up, too, and put my arms around her waist so that I could pull her close to me.

"Hey, I've got a great idea," I said. She looked up at me with those big, wide eyes. Sometimes I forget that Flan is still only in eighth grade, but when she looks at me like that, I remember. "Why don't we blow off the beginning of the party and go over to the Corner Bistro for burgers. It'll be like a great high culture–low culture contrast, and then we can show up fashionably late and everyone will wonder where we've been."

"Okay," Flan said, smiling indulgently at me. "That sounds like fun."

Then we started making out, and it was another half hour before we made it down to lower Fifth Ave, where my apartment is, and hailed a cab.

It was the perfect night for a party; there had been rain earlier in the day, and everything seemed fresh and bright and springlike. It felt good to be alone with Flan before throwing myself back into the big Manhattan night with its many social obligations.

I had a feeling I might enjoy this night a little *too* much.

"Yo, Davey, get me another hit of champagne," Arno Wildenburger yelled out, way too loud. Arno was six-one, half Brazilian and half German, and (everybody agreed) stunningly gorgeous. He was hard to miss, even when he wasn't bringing extra attention to himself.

The well-heeled art world crowd, mingling in the vast white-walled lobby of the MoMA, looked at him for a long, disapproving moment, and then the tinkling piano and light chatter resumed. Arno saw his mother whisper something into the ear of whatever socialite dowager she'd been talking up, and then whisk her to another side of the room. David Grobart took two glasses of champagne from a passing waiter and moved over to where Arno was standing.

"Thanks, man," Arno said, smiling to himself. David nodded and looked out at the crowd like it scared him.

It was the opening night of the big Luc Vogel retrospective, and pretty much everyone Arno knew was there. His parents were the famous Wildenburger art dealers, and Luc Vogel was one of their most famous clients. All of his parents' friends and enemies had turned out. A lot of kids that Arno knew were there, too, because his parents had enlisted his help in getting more of a "youthful crowd." Suited art world types were now mixing with beautiful young people in ripped designer clothes.

The Wildenburgers had thrown a pre-opening cocktail party for business associates and friends of the artist at their Chelsea town house, so Arno had already done his requisite mingling and was feeling a little restless. In fact, he was feeling more than restless. He was feeling like stirring up some trouble. It was a big night for his parents, and they were doing their power couple routine, in spite of the fact that they'd recently (and very publicly) decided to separate. It was annoying, really.

"Your mom looks different," David said absently. "Did she get something done?"

"Yeah, probably. Whatever," Arno said. "Let's find Rob and turn this party up a notch."

Arno gave a nod to the girl he'd been talking to, and he and David wandered through the lobby and up the great stone steps to the second floor mezzanine. The Luc Vogel stuff was all in the galleries up there, although nobody seemed to be bothering to look at it. Arno shrugged at David, and they moved from one huge print to another: a crowd of naked people lying in a field, a crowd of naked people crossing the Brooklyn Bridge, a crowd of naked people lying around the Wildenburger gallery.

"Do you think these people model professionally?" David asked.

Arno gave him a look. "Does it look like they do? I don't think so, David."

All that flesh looked very pink against the austere backgrounds, and there was something more hippy and childlike than adult and sexy about the people in the pictures. David nodded to show Arno that he got it.

"Eh, my brothers!" David and Arno turned and saw Rob coming toward them. His voice sounded even louder in the massive gallery with its soaring ceilings and monumental art.

Rob disappeared momentarily behind a gigantic, obelisk-like sculpture in the middle of the gallery, and then reappeared on the other side. He had a big smile on his face, and a blonde under each arm. Trailing behind them was a third, equally blond, girl. Arno recognized them from parties and around; they were that sleek, Upper East Side breed of girls, the kind who spent their weekends at charity balls or in East Hampton. They showed up in the society pages, too, either for being very reckless or for being very well-dressed, but

Arno was pretty sure he'd met these girls in person at least a couple of times. They all had perfect ski jump noses, and long, slightly bleached out, straightened hair. "David Grobart, Arno Wildenburger, meet Mimi, Lizzie, and Sadie. They are so wild!"

Arno kissed each girl on the cheek. David nodded at them awkwardly.

"You girls having a good time?" Arno asked.

They all nodded at once.

"I've been a Luc Vogel fan since I was, like, eleven," Mimi said with a sigh. She had one of those little girl voices that were kind of creepy and kind of hot at once. "That's when my parents bought me *#65/The Mall* for my bedroom in Jackson Hole. I love what his work says about the human body."

"Isn't she *del fuego*?" Rob cried.

Arno smiled rakishly. "You know, my parents represent Luc. I could, you know, introduce you to him if you want . . ."

"Really? That would be *such* an honor."

"Sure." Arno shrugged. "Should we go downstairs and mingle?"

"Yes! Let's go party," Rob said animatedly, "and drink more champagne."

They looked over the glass railing and down on the crowd in the lobby. The DJ had started, and the tinkling piano had finally been replaced by Old Dirty Bastard. The crowd had swelled, and people were starting to dance. Arno felt Mimi kind of swaying next to him, like she felt like dancing, too. He'd sworn off uptown girls after this very, *very* uptown girl named Liesel had turned out to be a total nightmare of a person last fall, but he had to admit that he kind of liked the way Mimi was moving.

Mimi was the tallest of the girls, and she seemed to be in charge. She was one of these girls with a permanent tan, an impossibly thin physique, and the confidence of a thirty-year-old. Mimi Rathbone—*that* was her name. Arno remembered reading something about her in Page Six recently. He was trying to think of what it had been, but looking at her in that incredibly low-cut dress right then, he was having trouble remembering much of anything. . . .

Rob put his arm around the waist of the girl with the high ponytail—her name was Lizzie—and headed for the stairs, and Arno kept his hand near the small of Mimi's back as they followed. David was left to figure out how best to negotiate Sadie. Arno wasn't sure why he thought Sadie was best for David, but she did seem like the least likely to bite. Maybe because of her cutesy Betty Page bangs? As they came down into the lobby, people turned their heads to look. Arno reflected, for a

13

moment, what good backup guys Rob and David made. They were both as tall and dark-haired as he was, and he could tell by the way people were staring that they looked frighteningly good with the uptown girls on their arms.

They moved into the crowd and started dancing. Everyone seemed to be having a good time, Arno thought, giving himself a little inward thumbs-up. Even David was admirably trying to dance, if you could call his shuffle that. Mimi had her arms draped around Arno's waist, and she was dancing pretty close to him. As a rule, Arno was never surprised when girls were into him, but girls like Mimi, as a rule, never went with guys who were actually still in high school. He was a little bit surprised in spite of himself. He kept dancing with her until someone got up to make a speech, shushing the DJ and the crowd in the process.

It was his father, Alec Wildenburger. He was standing on a raised part of the floor, and behind him you could see the outdoor sculpture garden through big, glass windows, looking magical in the glow of the orange street lights. In his hands were a champagne glass and a knife, which he was tapping together.

"I hope the bright young things will excuse me for a few moments so that an old, dull fellow can say some words about one of the masters . . . ," he began in his

14

signature urbane drawl. "One of the masters, who, I might add, has kept my wife and me quite well fed for over a decade, and one of the masters who, it seems, characteristically, is hiding this evening . . ."

Arno looked at Rob, who was silently making the international gesture for "Let's Party" with his fists in the air. "This is fucking boring," Arno whispered, though perhaps not as quietly as he could have.

"Come out, Luc Vogel . . . ," Alec Wildenburger was saying. "Come out, come out wherever you are!"

"I think I saw where they are keeping the cham-pagne," Rob hissed. He was definitely being a little noisier than was socially acceptable. "Let's go get a bottle for all and start our own party!"

Arno shrugged at Mimi. "You coming with?"

She whipped her hair over her shoulder, and smiled knowingly. "I'll go just about anywhere with you, Arno Wildenburger," she said.

Arno smiled to himself again—she was so into him that she'd forgotten all about meeting the brilliant Luc Vogel.

Mickey Pardo got to the MoMA party just as Alec Wildenburger was finishing his speech, which was perfect timing as far as Mickey was concerned. Mickey's dad was Ricardo Pardo, the sculptor, and he was represented by the Wildenburgers, so Mickey had heard these speeches before. They sucked.

Mickey was squat and firey, just like his father, so he was instantly recognizable to the crowd of art-world insiders. They nodded at him with affectionate distaste. As Mr. Wildenburger disappeared into the crowd, the music came back on and people started dancing and talking and yelling. It actually looked like kind of a cool scene. Mickey growled sweetly at Philippa Frady, who was his girlfriend again that week.

She shook her head and looked at him sternly. Then he remembered that he had promised her there would be no outlandish behavior that night. Also, no yelling. He tried to give her a smile devoid of mischievousness, and she sighed and kissed him on the forehead.

Mickey and Philippa had been together (on and off) for a long time.

They had finally agreed last fall that they should just be friends, at least until they went to college, or reached some slightly more advanced stage of adulthood. Their relationship could get a little intense sometimes, and besides, their parents were very invested in breaking them up. But then they managed to be back on just in time for Valentine's Day.

"Do you see Jonathan or anybody?" Mickey asked. He adjusted his powder blue tuxedo jacket, which he was wearing over dickies cutoffs.

Philippa shook her head.

"Damn," Mickey said. "You'd think Arno would be at his own parents' party, right?"

"Oh, he's here," Philippa said. "He and Rob are probably just scamming on freshmen girls somewhere."

"Nah, Arno doesn't date freshmen anymore," Mickey said as they moved through the crowd. "Bad for his rep, apparently. Hey, why's everybody staring at us?"

"Because last week we were broken up. We're confusing their simple minds."

"Oh, right."

They moved toward the center of the lobby, Mickey craning his neck for at least *one* of his guys. "Oh, shit," he said suddenly, grabbing Philippa by the arm.

"What?"

"My dad," Mickey yelped, pulling Philippa in the opposite direction and into a nook off the main lobby.

"You haven't told them we're back on yet, have you?"

"No, shhh, that's just going to cause a lot of yelling," Mickey said. He turned to see where they'd ended up. "Oh, sweet. Buffet."

"Mickey, this makes me *really* mad," Philippa said. She was petite and pale and gorgeous, and when she got mad she seemed to be radiating pure heat from the core of her being. Mickey thought she was adorable when she got like this.

"C'mon," he pleaded. Then he turned and started heaping his plate with shrimp.

"Mickey, how could you do this! I had, like, the biggest, suckiest confession session with my parents, and now your parents are going to find out from my parents, and I'm going to look totally stupid!"

"Phil, you never look stupid," Mickey said earnestly.

"Besides, it's dishonest," Philippa went on. "My therapist and I were just talking about how the problem with our relationship is that it has a culture of dishonesty, and she's so *dead on*. Everything is based on total delusion between us!"

"It is not!" Mickey yelled. Everyone else at the buffet table looked at them. The waiters cleared their throats.

18

"Besides, my therapist says we temper each others' worst qualities."

"Oh, that is such *bull*sh—," Philippa started to say.

"Excuse me—," someone said. They whipped their heads around. A girl with layered brown hair was standing next to them. She was holding a plate, and looked about twenty-five. In a voice slightly louder than everyone else's, and slow, like she was talking to the feeble-minded, she said: "Sorry to interrupt, but are you Mickey Pardo, son of the sculptor Ricardo Pardo?"

"Who are you?" Philippa asked coldly.

"Justine Gray, *New York* magazine," she said, wiping her hand on her jeans and extending her hand. "I'm a writer, and I'm here doing some last-minute research for our annual 'Hottest Private School Boy' issue. I was actually hoping I could talk to you."

Philippa held up a perfectly manicured hand, but Mickey was ready for some fun. He knew this issue. It came out every year, and Jonathan always read and talked about it obsessively.

"I'm hot," Mickey said. "I go to private school."

"Mickey," Philippa said. Mickey ignored her.

"This is my girlfriend, Philippa. She's hot, too. We're what you call a hot couple."

"Mickey—"

"See, the thing is, our parents don't want us to see

each other. But we can't be kept apart. That's how hot we are. We're practically about to burn this house down. We're Romeo and freaking Juliet. I mean, we've been going out since freshman year, and it's never been easy. But that's what makes it so worth it. It shouldn't *matter* whether my parents know we're back together. Right? *Right!?*"

"Uh-huh," the Gray girl said, politely pretending to take notes on a pad of paper.

"What else do you want to know about me?" Mickey asked, popping a shrimp in his mouth.

"*Mickey*," Philippa hissed, dragging him across the room. "Can I talk to you over here, please?" When they were a safe distance from the reporter person, she said, "You *do not,* I repeat *do not* tell my personal shit to random strangers. Is this what going out with you is always going to be like?!"

"*Phil*—"

"I'd hate to think my parents were right about something," she said pointedly. "Good-bye, Mickey."

Mickey watched Philippa walk back across the fabulous lobby, and then turned sheepishly back to the writer. Luckily, she was now engrossed in a cell phone conversation, and staring at the ceiling as she talked. Mickey darted into the adjoining nook.

He found himself in a small room that had been set

up like a lounge, with couches and ashtrays. There was only one dude, sitting and chomping a cigar, and Mickey sat down heavily beside him.

"What's your problem?" The man asked, not unkindly. He was on the smallish side and had downy blond hair, even though he was definitely at least forty.

"Fight with my girlfriend," Mickey muttered. He really didn't want to talk about it, even though talking about it with a stranger was, in a way, preferable to talking about it with his therapist. The chances that he would be asked to describe how it had made him *feel* were infinitely reduced.

"Eh, happens," the man said.

"What's *your* problem?" Mickey asked, irritated that his truly big problem would be dismissed so easily.

"Eh, you know, average midlife crisis stuff. You have a career retrospective of your work at the Museum of Modern Art, but what do you really *have*?"

"Luc Vogel?" Mickey said. "Mickey Pardo."

"Ricardo Pardo's boy?"

"You got it."

"Old devil, I should have known. You look just like him. We went to grad school together, you know," Luc Vogel said, passing Mickey his flask.

"Yeah, I know," Mickey took a long sip from the flask. Ah, tequila. "Listen, Luc, I think you're being kind of a wuss. Last I checked you were rich and famous. I mean, what could possibly be missing?"

"Well . . ." Luc Vogel cleared his throat in an attempt at modesty. "Not much, it's true. . . ."

"Anything . . . ?"

"I'm having a hard time coming up with . . ."

"*Nuthin'* . . . ?"

"Well, I have always wanted to do a nude crowd scene in a restaurant. There would be something so urbane about that, don't you think? Something lacking in the rest of my oeuvre . . . sort of Roman, but sort of bourgeois bohemian, too. But people never want to do that. Sanitary issues, I guess."

"That's what's missing?" Mickey asked incredulously.

"Yes, that's it." Luc Vogel stood up. He seemed satisfied.

"I think you could probably handle it if you wanted to," Mickey said, taking another swig of the tequila and passing it back.

"No, no, I have far too many projects already . . . ," the older man said, moving quickly toward the door. "Too many projects . . . No, I couldn't possibly . . . ," he went on vaguely. When he reached the door, he turned to Mickey, and smiled. "But you seem like quite the audacious young man. Set it up. I *dare* you."

He tossed the flask back to Mickey and was gone.

Patch Flood spent Thursday afternoon flipping through vinyl at A-1 Records on 6th Street and Avenue A, and now he was lying on his bed and listening to the classic T-Rex album he'd found. His cell was ringing again, so he closed his eyes. Patch wasn't really a cell phone kind of guy; his family had lived on a sailboat until they moved to their Perry Street townhouse when he was six. But Jonathan had insisted he get one a few years back, and since Jonathan did kind of freak out when he couldn't get in contact with his friends, Patch figured it was probably the brotherly thing to do.

That didn't mean he picked up his phone most of the time, of course. Patch was tall and sandy-haired and not easily excited or put out by stuff, so girls were always getting infatuated with him and calling him up nonstop. But the phone had been a particular pain in the ass today.

After the record store, he'd gone skateboarding in the basketball courts in Tompkins Square Park. He was watching some twenty-five-year-old totally blow it on his kick flip, when the cell rang three times in a row. Simon, this gutter kid whom Patch hung out with there sometimes, had been sitting next to him on the bench, and he took the phone out of Patch's pocket and said hello. Then he handed it to Patch and said, "It's for you, dude."

Patch took the phone and asked what was up.

"Hi, this is Justine Gray from *New York* magazine, and I wanted to—"

"Sorry, not interested." Patch hung up and shrugged at Simon. "Someone wanted to sell me a magazine subscription," he said.

The same number showed up in the caller ID window of his phone about once every ten minutes for the rest of the afternoon. He couldn't figure out why someone at *New York* would be trying to call him, but he disliked them on principle because *New York* had published a kind of nasty article about this girl Selina Trieff he used to go out with, about how she was out of control and trashed hotel rooms and stuff. It was supposedly about the rise of teen drinking, but she was the only kid they talked to. They had run a picture of her passed out on the couch with the headline WASTED BEAUTY?

Patch turned up the T-Rex and put a pillow over his head. His phone started making a noise a lot like the chorus of "Stayin' Alive." It stopped and started again. He picked it up, prepared to hurl it across the room. Then he remembered that Jonathan had assigned his number a special disco ring in Patch's phone so that Patch would know to pick up.

"J," Patch said.

"Hey, man, where are you?" Jonathan sounded tense, and there were definitely a lot of people in the background.

"Home. Why?"

"Because tonight's the Luc Vogel retrospective. How could you not be here?"

"I dunno. I'm kind of not crazy about the stuff of his we have in the house, so . . ." Patch trailed off.

"It's, like, a huge party at the MoMA, dude. Arno's parents are hosting it. You so should be here. We all agreed months ago we would come to this thing."

"I just forgot, I guess."

"Well, listen, Rob, Arno, and David are running around like a goddamn boy band with bottles of champagne and these skanky uptown girls, and Mickey's nowhere to be found, and . . ."

"Is Flan there?"

"Yeah, she says hi. And that you should be here. I really don't think I can take more of Rob, Arno, and David's eurotrash extravaganza without backup."

"Yeah, okay. I'm just gonna . . ."

"Patch? Hold on a sec, I have a call waiting . . ."

Patch stood up and wondered where he might have left his shirt. He stretched, twisting his long, lean torso right and left, and thought about whether a shower was absolutely necessary before this party thing. Then Jonathan came back on.

"Dude, I have to take this call. But you're on your way, right?"

"Yeah, okay," Patch said, and hung up.

His phone flashed him a message that he had twenty-seven unopened voicemails.

i get a whiff of that ol' fame and glory

I got off the phone with Patch and switched back to the other line. It was this girl who worked at *New York*, Justine Gray. She hadn't told me why she was calling yet, but I was pretty sure I knew what it was about.

"So talk to me. What's up?" I said.

"Hi, Jonathan. Like I said, I'm a writer for *New York* magazine, and I'm working on an article about *the coolest* of cool private school boys. Obviously, you're pretty well known for your taste and all that. I was hoping I could get some quotes from you for the article."

I looked over at Flan. Her arms were crossed, and she was looking at the ceiling. Pretty much everyone was on the dance floor, which was where she wanted to be. I knew this. But I'd felt weird when we were out there before—Rob and Arno were on the dance floor, too, and kind of making a scene with these three blondes who are juniors at Florence. Flan goes to Florence, too, and the older girls kept giving Flan looks like they were wondering what she was doing out so late on a school night. It was really irritating me. Plus, Rob kept yelling foreign words, which is just something nobody should have to put up with.

"Yeah, I've read your stuff," I said into the phone. "I'd be happy to be interviewed. When's good for you?"

"Well, my deadline's tomorrow."

"Oh. I'm at the Luc Vogel opening right now, but . . ."

"I know. Me, too. I'm over by the buffet table. How about now?"

I looked over toward the room with the buffet table and saw someone waving at me.

"Absolutely," I said, trying to hide my enthusiasm since I knew this Justine person was obviously working on the Hottest Private School Boy issue. They've done it eight years in a row now, and it is a huge deal. The guy they pick is on the cover, and they write this very puffy piece about what makes him so hot, with pictures and all that. This issue has *made* people. The inaugural Hottest Private School Boy was Tyler Ash, who was a senior at Gissing then. He dropped out of Yale his sophomore year and traveled around, and now he writes for *Saturday Night Live*. You've probably seen his name in Page Six, because he is frequently caught canoodling with the female hosts at Lotus or some other place like that after the show.

Most private school guys in Manhattan are supposed to go to good colleges, and most of the HPSBs have. But last year's, Danny Abraham, didn't even bother. He started a nightclub called Ginger as soon as he graduated high school, and it's done very well. You've probably heard of Ginger, too; it's one of those places everybody goes to, but nobody can get into.

Heard of Black-Jack-Point front man Orlando Simenon? Yeah, he was one, too.

So, Hottest Private School Boy is a very big deal, and I would be lying if I said I wasn't thinking that maybe I'd been chosen. I was even praying for it pretty hard, since I've heard designers start sending you clothes as soon as the issue hits the stands, on top of everything else.

Justine Gray was still waving at me. I waved back and hung up, and then I turned to Flan.

"Hey, gorgeous . . ."

"Who were you talking to?" she asked.

I tried to make a sighing noise to indicate that it was all very irritating, rather than totally exciting. Flan was not going to like being left alone in the middle of a party. "This . . . person from *New York* magazine. They want to interview me, I don't know, something about the scene with private school kids now, you know the type of thing. So I'm gonna have to go now. But I'll find you in a little while, okay?"

"*Jonathan*," she said, her eyes widening, "you cannot ditch me here."

"I'm not *ditching* you."

"Oh yeah? What do you call leaving me alone in a room full of strange people who are older than I am?" she asked.

"Flan, this is important."

"Why? You just made it sound like a big bore."

This time I sighed for real. "You remember last year when the Hottest Private School Boy issue came out, with Danny Abraham on the cover?"

"Uh-huh."

"Well, they do it every spring. I think that's what this is for, and . . . listen, Flan, if they want to name me Hottest Private School Boy in New York, I really can't say no. You know?"

I kissed her on the cheek, and then I walked over

to the buffet room. The girl who had waved at me was still standing there, waiting. She was wearing a knockoff Chanel jacket and Seven jeans, with a very wide belt and very pointy shoes. She looked pretty hopped up. I tried not to show how excited I was when I introduced myself.

"I'm *so* honored to meet you," she said loudly. "I think there's a lounge over there. Does that sound like a good place to sit and talk? I want to find out what makes Jonathan tick."

Okay, who would say something like that to anyone but New York's Hottest Private School Boy? I was *so* in. I nodded like I didn't care at all.

As I followed Justine to the lounge rooms, I turned to see how Flan was doing without me. She was standing against the wall where I'd left her with her arms crossed. She looked uncomfortable, and a little pissed. *She'll thank me when I'm the Hottest Private School Boy*, I thought, and turned back to follow Justine.

"Woohooo!" someone shouted, pretty close to David Grobart's ear. It was his friend Rob Santana, who was doing something that looked like dancing, except dirtier, with one of the three blondes he and Arno had picked up. Rob stuck his tongue out in David's direction and then made another whooping noise. David was doing something like dancing, too, although it was the kind of quasi-dancing that guys like him resorted to only when they really had to. He moved his long limbs around to the beat, approximately.

David was six-four, and he played basketball for Potterton. He was more of a hoodie-and-sneakers guy than an art world guy, but he was doing his best to follow Rob's lead. After all, Rob had been his friend when all his New York guys forgot about him. Plus, the MoMA party that night was a big deal for Arno, whom David had also been spending a lot of time with lately. This seemed like a good thing, because he and Arno had had some beef over the years, like when Arno made out with David's girlfriend, Amanda Harrison-Deutschmann, last fall. David's parents said it was wonderful they had grown so close again, and that it was an excellent healing process. David's parents were therapists.

Still, David was having a hard time keeping up with Rob and Arno tonight. For one thing, he was pretty sure that Rob had just yelled "I love you, MAMI!" really loud, and for another, the girls they were hanging out with were a little intimidating. They were all physically small, the same shade of blond, and they all had this sort of plastic sheen over their skin. Their noses all ski-jumped in exactly the same way. They were like Amanda Harrison-Deutschmann times fifteen. And there were three of them.

He was also having a hard time telling them apart, because they were so similar-looking. *Could they be sisters or something?* David wondered.

"I have to pee," said the blonde he was dancing with. Was her name Bunny? It was something like that. She was the one with bangs.

"Okay," David said, trying not to look relieved. "I'll walk you to the bathroom."

They waved at Rob, who had his face sunk deep into Bunny II's neck. Nobody noticed as they walked away from the dance floor.

When they got to the bathroom, David looked around awkwardly. Was he supposed to wait for her? He hoped not.

"See ya," the girl said. Had she interpreted David's awkwardness as a lack of interest? Now, that would make him feel bad. David decided that he really was going to have to learn how to handle girls liking him better, now that he was hanging with Rob and Arno all the time. He just didn't know how to disentangle himself the way they did.

"Um, I kind of forgot your . . ."

"Sadie," she said. There was a little irritation in her voice. She pointed at herself, and spoke in a Neanderthal voice: "Me, Sadie. I'll see you later, David." And then she strode into the bathroom with her purse thrown over her shoulder. David looked at her legs and wondered if they really made skirts that short, or if you had to have them altered.

David waited a minute and then, not knowing what else to do, wandered into a nearby room. He saw that it was a coat check room converted into a bar, and it was spare and dark and lit mostly by candles. Mickey was leaning up against the bar. He was holding a beer and talking to some girl who was not Philippa. As David came up behind them, he heard Mickey saying: "Yeah, that's what the dude said."

"But in a *restaurant*?" the girl replied, wrinkling her nose and dropping her bottom lip. "Isn't that sort of, um, nasty?"

"Hey, Mickey," David said.

"Oh, hey, dude. What up," Mickey said. They gave each other an awkward, back-slapping hello hug.

"What's up with you?" David asked. He was feeling a little light-headed from the champagne, so he ordered a Red Stripe.

"Nothing . . . ," Mickey said, swigging from his own beer. He looked like it wasn't his first drink, either. In fact, he looked a little crazed.

The girl he'd been talking to made an *ahem* noise. "So, tell me what Luc Vogel's like, though . . . ," she said.

"Who cares about that?" Mickey said, dropping the empty beer on the ground, and kicking it, soccerlike, across the floor. Luckily, his beer had come in a can. Mickey turned back to the girl and said, "Do you want to get drunk with me?"

David inched backward away from Mickey, who was obviously on a tear of some kind tonight. David had gotten caught up in a Mickey tear before, and he wasn't looking to do that again right now. As he inched along the wall, he saw the blonde (Sadie? That's what she'd said, right?) coming out of the bathroom. She tossed her hair over her shoulder and pointed her ski jump nose in the air. David tried to disappear as much as a guy of his size can, and crouched down very low. The blonde walked straight back to the dance floor.

David was still instinctively hunched, and looking warily out at the crowd at about waist level, when he noticed something strange. There was a girl about ten feet in front of him wearing one of those dramatic, open-back dresses that go so low they almost reveal an unladylike crack, but don't. And just to the left of the small of her back, there was something large and black. Was it a giant fly? David moved closer.

The black thing was definitely big, and frightening. What was it doing in such a delicate area? David had a brochure of the Luc Vogel show in his hand; he rolled it, lifted it, and brought it down with a loud smack on the black spot. That lovely back twisted around in his direction, but the black spot stayed put.

"Excuse me," the girl in the low-back dress said. She had a slightly husky, sardonic kind of voice.

Why, David asked himself, was he always doing the most moronic shit?

"Uh, I'm sorry. You had a bug on your back, I think," David said, sounding stupider than even he could have imagined. "Maybe it was a fly?"

She opened her mouth and laughed. "That's a mole, jerk," she said. She said it kind of nicely, David thought.

She was weird looking, with big almond eyes, a twisted nose with a bump halfway down, a tiny, puckered mouth, and an unbelievably long neck.

"Oh," David said. He realized she looked like the Modigliani painting he'd just seen hanging in one of the upstairs galleries; she had the blocky, exotic features that the great moderns all had been obsessed with. (He had just read that off a gallery wall.) David couldn't stop staring at her.

"You're sorry?" the girl said. He thought her eyes kind of glittered when she said that.

"Yeah," he said. "Really, really sorry."

She looked over her shoulder at the group of friends she had been standing with. "Those are my friends. Sorry," she said. Then she bit her lip, like she was waiting for something to happen.

"Hey . . . do you wanna get out of here, maybe?" David couldn't believe he'd just said that. He sounded like Arno. But somehow he knew he liked this girl.

She smiled big. Was that the beginning of a nod? David could feel the *yes* coming like the best sneeze ever. And then he saw, over the Modigliani girl's shoulder, something that made his heart sink. It was Rob and Arno and the three very blond girls, charging in his direction. There was somebody else with them, too. A girl with a notepad.

David knew they were coming for him.

Arno spotted David and threw his hand in the air. "Yo, Davey," he yelled.

David was standing next to a girl with a kind of weird face—her features were all big and wrong somehow. When Arno got over to them, he tried to ignore the fact that David had been talking to her.

"Hey, dude," Arno said. "You ready to blow?"

David shrugged and looked at the girl next to him.

"Great," Arno said. "We're going to that party at Lotus, the one that Jonathan got us all on the list for? But first I want you to meet Justine." Arno gestured at the *New York* writer he'd just met, and then at David. "David plays ball for Potterton," he went on.

"Nice to meet you," Justine said, shaking David's hand. David nodded and looked over his shoulder. The girl with the funny face had taken Arno's hint and disappeared back into the crowd.

"Um, yeah. I'm not quite ready to go yet," David said.

They were pretty far from the dance floor now, but Rob had started dancing with both Mimi and Lizzie again. Sadie was texting someone. Arno could feel himself getting annoyed: He had had enough of the MoMA and wanted to go somewhere else now, and he didn't understand why David was making things hard for him. "David," he said, putting his arm around David's shoulder. "Let's talk."

They moved away from Rob, the blondes, and Justine.

"You okay?"

"Um, yeah," David said, still kind of looking around expectantly.

"That girl Justine wants to talk to you," Arno said.

"I think she's a little old for me," David said. He clearly was not paying attention.

"No shit. She's a writer for a magazine. She wants to talk to you for this story she's working on."

"Oh."

"So . . . could you talk to her?" Arno asked. "And then we'll go? I think this party at Lotus is going to give her some really great material."

"Why does she want to talk to me?" David asked.

"'Cause she's writing about cool New York kids,

39

which I *thought* you were." Arno sighed. It was tough sometimes, how people didn't think the same way he did. "She needs some quotes, dude."

David gave him a pained expression. "I'm not going to have anything to say," he said. In fact, he sort of whined it.

"David, come on, freaking help me out here," Arno said. "Look, can you keep a secret? You know the Hottest Private School Boy issue *New York* does every year?"

David nodded.

"Well, that's what she's working on. And this year, you know who it's gonna be?"

David shook his head. Arno was smiling big.

"Me."

patch overhears something
he definitely shouldn't

Patch could be sad. He knew he could, because he was sad right now.

He had walked all the way from his house on Perry Street to the MoMA, off Fifth Avenue in Midtown, which was actually a pretty far walk. He had taken a little detour through Union Square, because it was a nice night: The air was moist and warm, and there were people everywhere, yelling and laughing and traveling in packs. He liked Union Square, too, because people sat around eating ice cream there, or went skateboarding, or picnicked late at night with people they really cared about. But when he crossed 18th Street and got back onto Fifth, his phone rang again and then made an annoying buzzing noise telling him that he had a message. He figured he'd better listen to it. Or, actually, he figured he'd better listen to at least a few of the many messages he'd ignored already today.

The first one went like this:

"Hey, Patch, this is Justine Gray at *New York* magazine. I'm writing a story about cool kids in New York, and I was hoping you'd be one of my sources. Could you call me back so that we can set up an interview? I'd appreciate it. Thanks."

The next five said more or less the same thing, except the girl's voice got increasingly urgent, like she'd had a little too much coffee, or maybe something stronger and synthetic. Patch erased them all, as well as a message from his little sister, Flan, reminding him about the party and telling him that she really wanted him there. Then he listened to yet another message from Justine Gray.

"Hi, Patch, this is Justine again from *New York*. Wow, I feel like I *know* you from hearing your voice on the outgoing message so many times. But I don't really, and Patch, I'd like to. *New York* would like to. So: I'm going to put all my cards on the table. We want you to be the Hottest Private School Boy in New York for our HPSB 2005 issue. We've talked to a lot of people, and the consensus is, *you* are probably the coolest person ever to attend a private school in Manhattan. What makes you so cool? You don't *need* anything, and you don't *want* anything. That's what the people say. You're an island, Patch Flood, a very cool island unto yourself."

Patch hung up without listening to any more. His phone made a buzzing noise, and flashed him a note that he still had twenty unopened messages. What did that mean, *an island*? He figured there was no way he was listening to twenty more bullshit messages like that one, so he tossed the phone over his shoulder and kept walking.

But when he got to MoMA, he was still thinking about that message and what it said. If that was true, that thing about him not wanting anything, then that was really, really sad. He knew she was wrong. He *knew* there were things he wanted and needed . . . he just wasn't sure what they were.

When he came into the grand lobby of the new MoMA, the party was still going strong, but he couldn't see anybody he really wanted to talk to. He walked through the crowd of kids—all the grown-up art world people had split long ago—and looked around. There had to be *someone* he wanted to talk to.

"Patch!" yelled a voice from behind him.

Patch turned and saw Jonathan. They slapped each other five, and nodded hello.

"What's up, J? You having a good time?"

"I was, but . . ." Jonathan paused, like he was trying to think of the best way to say something he really didn't want to say. He was wearing a suit, and he looked more dressed up than anybody else in the room. "Um, listen, I think your sister's mad at me."

"Why would she be mad at you?"

"I don't know. She's been in the bathroom for, like, an hour."

"Why would she be in there?" Patch gave his friend a long, stormy-green-eyed stare. That usually got him talking.

"See, I got this call from this woman who's a reporter for *New York*, and she's working on the Hottest Private School Boy issue, which is . . . never mind, anyway, she wanted to interview me, for a story that I'm *pretty sure* is about me, so . . . I guess I kind of left Flan alone a little too long while I was talking to her. The magazine lady, I mean."

"Oh." Patch sunk his hands into the pair of worn khakis, rolled to the knees, that he'd been wearing all day. He was pretty sure Jonathan was not going to be the HPSB, and he was equally sure that he didn't want to be the one to tell him.

"Yeah," Jonathan sighed, "I know. I'm a lame boy-friend. But could you maybe talk to her?"

Patch nodded. He wanted to get away from Jonathan as quickly as he could right then. Patch did not like lying to his friends, and not telling Jonathan about the messages he'd gotten felt a lot like lying. "Yeah, man. I'll talk to her."

"Hey," Jonathan said, "there's a party at Lotus later

that this ex-girlfriend of my brother is throwing. She put us all on the list, if you want to go."

Patch shrugged. "We'll see," he said, and walked through the crowds of slightly buzzed kids to the women's bathroom.

He knocked on the door and listened. When no one answered, he knocked again and went in. There was nobody at the mirror, and he walked along the stalls, looking underneath the stall doors for feet. He didn't see any until he got to the last one, where he saw a familiar pair of white Marc Jacobs boots.

"Hey, Flan, it's me," he said.

"Patch?"

"Yup."

He heard the lock pulling back, and then Flan peeked around the stall door looking very forlorn indeed. Her eye makeup was all smudged down her cheeks. She went back and sat on the top of the toilet.

"What's the matter, kiddo?" Patch asked. He came in and closed the stall door behind him. He slid down it and sat cross-legged on the floor. "C'mon," he said. "Talk to me."

"Oh, it's nothing, really . . ." Flan mumbled.

Patch tilted his head and gave her a look.

"Jonathan is just . . . It's like he doesn't care about me *at all*," she said, looking at her brother.

"Flannie, that sounds sort of stupid. Jonathan totally cares about you."

"I know but, it's like there are always these things he *has* to do, and I subsequently *have* to do. I mean, I have friends, too. It's just like he doesn't even think about that, or what I might have given up to come out with him tonight. Or any night. You know what I mean?"

Patch nodded and brushed the hair out of his eyes. "That's what J's like, though, Flannie, like a social director or something. He feels obligated, I guess. But talk to him about it. He's crazy about you. Sometimes people can change each other for the better, you know?"

Patch wondered if what he had just said were true. Flan sniffled.

"Tissue?" Patch asked, pulling on the toilet paper roll, and handing a wad of it to Flan.

"Shut up, bitch!" A voice shrieked.

Flan and Patch looked up. Someone had just come into the women's room, banging the door against the wall. In fact, there were three of them, and they were all busting up laughing now, at three distinct, girly pitches.

"No, really—I think you've gained. You have total carb face."

"You are *such* a ho."

"I'm just *kidding*, Sadie. It was, like, a *joke*."

There was silence for a moment, and Patch moved as

quietly as he could away from the stall door. He gave his little sister a *what's going on?* look, and she mouthed "makeup" back at him.

"Lizzie, can I use your mascara?"

"That's disgusting. You *know* you aren't supposed to share mascara."

"Come the fuck on."

"Fine."

More silence. Then:

"So, you think she's shitting him, or is he really going to be Hottest Private School Boy?"

"I can see it."

"Yeah, I can totally see it."

"This is so cool that we're hanging with the next Hottest Private School Boy."

"Totally. We should do something. Like, get 'Mrs. Wildenburger' T-shirts printed up or something."

"Yeah!"

"No, something bigger."

"Bigger?"

"Yeah, like . . . let's have a little competition to see who can hook up with him the most while he's still on the newsstands. Whoever hooks up with Arno the most, wins."

There was some embarrassed giggling on the other side of the women's room.

"Could we do that? Mimi, that's hot."

"Wait, like *really* hook up with him?"

"Sadie, you are such a goddamn sissy. Are you my friend or not?"

"Fine, I'm in. Whatever."

"This is major. Okay, ground rules. We all keep our own score on the honor system. None of us can act like we know he's hooked up with another one of us. Anyone who tries to get him to go out exclusively loses automatically. And no action till he's actually on the newsstand."

"Pinkie swear," all three voices said at once.

Patch looked at Flan. She was miming "gag me."

"All right, ladies," the loudest, bitchiest voice said. "You look killer. Let's rock."

Patch listened to them file out, and then he stood up.

"Skanks," Flan said disgustedly, standing up, too.

"Hey, you feeling any better?"

"Yes, big brother. Thank you for talking."

"Are you going to go find Jonathan?" Patch asked.

"Uh-huh."

"Okay, good. But first, *swear* to me you will not tell anybody what we just heard."

"Um, sure," Flan said.

"*Especially* Jonathan."

"Okay."

"Do you swear?"

Flan looked up at him with her big round eyes. "I swear."

"Jonathan, what are you doing?"

I turned and saw Arno leaning against the wall next to me. David was coming up behind him, and Justine, the *New York* reporter, was right there, too. It seemed like Justine was shadowing my guys, which was probably a good idea—I mean, you can't be HPSB-hot without a great crew behind you, right?

I hadn't been doing anything but waiting for Flan to not be mad at me anymore, so I just said, "What's up."

"Nothing, man," Arno said. "Did you meet Justine?"

"Yeah, hi again."

"Sorry we got interrupted earlier," she said effusively. "*Nothing* could have torn me away from that conversation. But it was the office, and they own me."

I shrugged. "No biggie," I said.

That actually didn't sound like the kind of phrase an HPSB would use, but Justine was staring at me so enthusiastically that I figured I could probably fall on my face and she would still want me on the cover of her magazine. I was so sure of my title right then that I started mentally planning a party for Monday night to celebrate the release of my HPSB issue.

Then she took out a digital camera and started taking pictures of me. I posed nonchalantly, and when she was done, she said, "Who did your suit? For the credits page, of course."

This was way too exciting. Before I could reply, the three blond Florence girls reinvaded my group. The leader of their pack, who wore her hair long and straight a la Blake Lively, draped herself over Arno and said, "Can we go now?" It took me a minute to recognize her as Mimi Rathbone, this girl I'd just read about in Page Six. Something about how she'd been making out with an actor who is practically her dad's age at Coral Room.

"Word," Arno said. Then he looked at me and said, "Hey, man, we're all going to that Lotus thing, right?"

"Totally," I said. "Oh, and by the way, on Monday I'm having a little party at my house to celebrate—" I looked at Justine, and paused, because I realized just in time that I shouldn't seem so sure in front of my profiler. I caught myself, and said, "You know, stuff," instead.

"Uh, cool," Arno said.

That was when I remembered about Flan, because that's when she came walking back from the bathroom with Patch. She looked like she'd been crying, but also happier, too. Still, her appearance suggested she might not be so up for Lotus.

"Hi, Flan," David said. I had forgotten he was there, he'd been so quiet. David's a good-looking guy, but he's not the smoothest. People forget about him more than they should. Patch man-braced Arno and David, whom I guess he hadn't seen yet tonight.

"You coming?" Arno asked him.

"Where?" Patch said.

"Lotus," Arno said. "Oh, by the way, this is Justine Gray from *New York*. She wants to see how the cool kids do it nowadays."

"You should come," Justine said.

"No, thanks," Patch said quickly. "I'm actually going to go home now."

"Ah, come on. It's going to be hot," Mimi said.

She winked at Patch lasciviously, and that was when I knew Lotus was definitely not going to be a Flan-appropriate evening.

After leaving my guys behind to get into whatever trouble they were going to find at Lotus, Flan and I got in a taxi and headed downtown, toward home. I love the way New York looks at night, speeding down an avenue in a cab. All the lights from the delis and the bars and the big buildings blur by, like at a carnival, while you sit in this kind of peaceful, quiet place. Tonight was even better because I had my girl's head resting on my shoulder.

Flan's hair was down now, and a little tangled, and it spread out over my chest. It smelled like lavender shampoo. Her body felt all tired and relaxed against me.

I was almost over not getting to go to Lotus, too. I'd told my guys and Justine that, on second thought, Lotus seemed kind of over to me now, but that it was cool they were going since I'd gotten them on the list and they could go for free. Then Flan had asked if I wanted to go over to her house and watch old movies, and that *did* actually sound kind of perfect.

"Jonathan?" she said.

"What's up, pretty?"

"Why do we fight so much?"

I brushed Flan's hair back behind her ear and smiled. "Because we're perfect for each other. That's why."

She smiled and snuggled more into me.

The fact that stuff with Flan was so good, and that I was going to be the next Hottest Private School Boy, had me pretty psyched. Also, I was consumed by the idea of my Monday night victory bash.

"You know," I said, "Wilmer Hadley, HPSB 2003, is living in Paris right now. They just did this follow-up article about him in *New York,* about how he's the central personality of the 'Nouveau Lost Generation,' or something like that."

I felt Flan kind of stiffen against me. I guess it made sense that she would be nervous about what would happen once I was basically named the hottest guy in Manhattan.

"You *love* Paris," I said. Then I realized that, if I wanted to be a good boyfriend, which I would like to be, I would address her concerns head on. "You know, when . . . I mean, *if* I'm named Hottest Private School Boy, it's not going to change things."

"Huh?" Flan said. I could tell she was uncomfortable.

"I mean, that whole thing with the reporter and all that. And I know that the HPSB issue can change lives. I just want you to know that it won't change us."

"Oh," Flan said. She stared out the window for a long, winsome moment. "Jonathan, the thing is . . ." She paused, like she was stopping herself from saying something. Then she blew on the window, and drew a heart in the foggy layer that she'd left there. "I just wish you didn't care so much about that article, that's all."

Wait, what did *that* mean?

"I don't. Whatever. It's totally not a big deal," I said defensively. "Oh, by the way, I'm having a party Monday night to celebrate, so cancel whatever you've got."

"I can't," Flan said. "That's the night Daria is having all the girls over for a sleepover."

"Flan, it's my HPSB party—you *have* to be there."

There was something like sadness in Flan's eyes when she nodded and said that of course she'd find a way to be there. I was worried there was going to be another fight, but then she kissed me, really softly at first. The cab was flying down Fifth, past my house and toward Perry Street. Everything felt really light and good, and the weekend had only just begun.

the boys leave messages all weekend long

"Wildenburger, talk to me." BEEP.

"Oooooo, my head! Arno, c'est moi, Rob, and it's Friday morning. Not going to school as I think I may still be drunk from last night. Tee hee! That was a party incredible last night, my friend, and we were, how you say, ruling. Cool that the reporter lady hung with us all night: don't think she'd seen anything like that before! Ai ai ai! Call me when you get up. Ciao."

"Hello, it is Rob. Bueno, es Rob. Allo, c'est Rob. Digame." BEEP.

"I feel like shit man. It's Arno. Were Mimi and Lizzie and Sadie there all night? I think I remember someone swinging from a chandelier . . . And were we hanging with the Backseat Rockstars' bassist? God, it's a blur. Any ideas, ring me. I'm having coffee with Justine for some last minute Qs, if you know what I mean. Oh, and have you talked to David yet? What's on for tonight? And Rob, do me a favor and change that fucking message."

Guitar solo in the background. Girl's voice says: "This is Mickey's phone. Go ahead and leave him a message, but don't be surprised if he doesn't call you back." BEEP.
"Hey, Mickey, it's J. I barely even saw you last night, man. Anyway, I just wanted to remind you that I'm having a party Monday night for . . . well, just be there. Like, nine-ish. Oh, and did you end up at the Lotus party?"

"Hi, you've reached the cell phone of Justine Gray. Leave your name, number, and the best time to call you, and I'll get back to you as soon as possible. Thanks a mil!" BEEP.
"Hey, Justine, it's Jonathan, you know, from the MoMA party. It's, like, one-thirty on Friday. I know our interview got cut short, and that you mentioned something about filing your story Friday afternoon. Anyway, just wanted to check in and see if there's anything you need. You know my number. Cool, bye."

"You've reached the Frady residence. Please leave your information after the beep, and we will return your call as promptly as possible." BEEP.
"Yo, it's Mickey. Is Philippa there? Philippa! I've left,

like, a million messages on your cell. Why won't you call me back? Are you still mad? Don't be mad. And call me. I'm in love with you!"

Guitar solo in the background. Girl's voice says: "This is Mickey's phone. Go ahead and leave him a message, but don't be surprised if he doesn't call you back." BEEP.
"Hey, Mickey, J again. Um, just wondering—did some chick named Justine talk to you? I was just wondering because I think she needs to talk to me again, and I wanted to see if you maybe knew a land line I could reach her at. Don't trip, call me when you get a chance."

"Wildenburger, talk to me." BEEP.
"You just called me. It's David, it's, like, eleven-thirty on Friday night, I'm right outside Marquee, and there's like an enormous line. I'll be in as soon as I can."

"Hi, um, this is David. Leave a message, and I'll get you back. Um, how do you? Mmph . . ." BEEP.
"Yo, Davey. Arno. It's, like, twelve-fifteen. Why are you at Marquee? We left there, like, an hour ago. We're at Milk and Honey now. Just get here, okay? Mimi and Lizzie are here, and they say Sadie's about to show up, so not only should you be here, you should really *want* to be here. Out."

"You've reached the Frady residence. Please leave your information after the beep, and we will return your call as promptly as possible." BEEP.

"Philippa, please please call me back? It's Mickey, obviously. Do you despise me? What is *up?*"

"Hi, this is Jonathan. Don't forget to leave your number if I don't have it."

"Jonathan, it's David and it's, like, noon on Saturday. I am at basketball practice and I feel like I'm going to barf. Could you please remind me not to stay out till four when I have practice the next day? Thanks. Oh, and I'm feeling a little vulnerable right now, and maybe that's what's doing the talking, but it's weird that we haven't been hanging lately. Um, bye."

"Hi! It's Flan. I miss you already, so leave me a message." BEEP.

"Flan, it's Jonathan. Sorry, I know I'm supposed to pick you up after riding class, but I'm running a little late because I was picking up stuff for Monday night. Wait for me, okay?"

Guitar solo in the background. Girl's voice says: "This is Mickey's phone. Go ahead and leave him a message, but don't be surprised if he doesn't call you back." BEEP.

"Hey, Mickey, it's Jonathan. It's Saturday, man. What's going on tonight? I'm trying to see if I can get something going. Let me know what you've got. Oh, and remind everyone about Monday, okay? Bye."

"Hi, this is Patch's new phone. You know the drill." BEEP. "Patch, it's Jonathan, it's, like, eight-thirty on Saturday night. I'm at your house, but you're not here. Are you around? Maybe we could get a beer. Later."

"You've reached the Frady residence. Please leave your information after the beep, and we will return your call as promptly as possible." BEEP. "Phiiiiiilllllllllllliiiiiiiipppppppppppppaaaaaaaaaaaaaa!!!!!!!!!"

"Wildenburger. Talk to me." BEEP. "Arno, it's David. Sunday night and I just left Don Hill's. Sorry I didn't say bye, but I couldn't find you and I've got school tomorrow. But call me then, okay? Oh, and did Jonathan invite you to some party tomorrow night?"

I'm assuming you all know what Monday morning feels like, so I won't bore you with the bummer
details. But I was feeling strangely good when I
woke up on this particular Monday. I don't know if
it was the residual glow of the MoMA party (which,
the more I thought about it, had been a really
classy kind of night), or maybe it was the mellow
weekend that Flan and I had shared, with lots of
movie watching and walks in the village and window shopping, rather than my usual excess of
drinking and lack of sleep. Although, I have to
admit, the anticipation of the new issue of *New
York* was probably key to my unusually sunny
mood.

I put on a pair of gray Calvin Klein slacks and a
yellow Kenneth Cole polo shirt, grabbed my
school stuff, and headed out. My mom has been
doing private Bikram yoga sessions from eight-
thirty to ten, five days a week, so I never really see

her in the mornings anymore. She swears it's improving her mood, though.

I waved to the doorman and the guy selling fruit on the corner, and Mrs. Bancroft, who was coming in from walking her Pekingese. We've had the apartment for a long, long time.

When I got to the Universal News stand on 14th street near Fifth, I was trying to be very casual. I mean, that's the way a Hottest Private School Boy *should* be—not too easily ruffled, you know what I mean? I looked at newspaper headlines and flipped absently through a few more news-oriented magazines. Then I saw it out of the corner of my eye, but what caught my attention wasn't even the fact that it was *New York* magazine, it was who was on the cover. I knew that face.

And it wasn't mine.

I moved, as calmly as possible, to the stack of *New York*s, and picked one up. The clerk was discussing some sort of political event with one of his customers, and so I slunk into the corner and braced myself for a real look. I looked that cover photo right in the eye.

My friend Arno Wildenburger was staring back at me, positioned jauntily in front of a dark kind of club scene. His brow was arched, the way it always is when he wants to convey that he gets a lot of girls, or that he knows more about vintage tennis shoes than you do, or something else like that. Lest the significance be lost on me (which was not really even a possibility at this point), the headline *Arno Wildenburger: The Hottest Private School Boy Manhattan Has Ever Seen?* was scrawled across his midsection.

I must have been staring at it kind of gape-mouthed for longer than I thought—to me, it felt like time was standing still—because the clerk started yelling at me.

"Hey, are you going to buy that or what?" he was saying when I finally looked up.

I didn't handle this gracefully, I'll admit. I put down the *New York,* and ran out of the Universal without saying anything.

When I got back onto the street (where it was a totally unfairly beautiful day) the whole Arno-as-HPSB thing seemed like a bad dream. It was totally possible—it was entirely possible—that this was a printing error. I mean, it was a weekly, and their star reporter was out getting tanked with teen-agers the night before she had to file her story. There were bound to be mix-ups, right?

I headed across Union Square toward the big

Hay & Royals there. You had to figure that, in all their corporate four-story glory, not a single printing error could make it in there. But by the time I charged through their doors, and stepped onto the escalator, I was feeling distinctly less optimistic.

The magazine aisle was full of kids ditching class and aspiring writers reading the table of contents of various obscure literary journals. I grabbed ten copies of *New York* and went to sit in the coffee area. I ordered a venti Americano, black, and found a relatively private table near the window. That way, if things got really shitty, I could always throw myself out of it.

Every single issue of *New York* had the same cover, the same table of contents, and worse yet, the same cover story complete with photographs of Arno, Rob, and David partying. One particularly unjust caption read, "Wildenburger and his friends get down at Lotus, where they are always on the list." What was this, *Star*? It was like pure fiction.

I got them on that list.

I mean, we're talking about Arno Wildenburger here. I've known the guy since I was, what, eight? He's good-looking, and girls trample all over each other to get a little attention from him, and the guy can dress. (I should know.) But the guy isn't a taste maker, and he's not the brightest bulb. (I should know that, too.)

I sipped my coffee and wished I could go back half an hour, to the person I was before I learned of this huge cosmic mistake. I decided there was no way I could handle school today, at least not until after noon. Then I called Patch. I guess I wanted sympathy, but when I heard his voice on the line I realized that he was not the person to understand about Hottest Private School Boy.

"What's up, J?" he said. He sounded a little down, too.

"I just wanted to see if you were cool," I said. "I mean, good. You went MIA this weekend, and that hasn't happened in a long time."

Patch didn't say anything for a minute, and then he thanked someone who wasn't me. "What? Jonathan? I'm fine. I'm just on the way to school, can I call you later?"

"Sure," I said. "We should hang out," I added, before clicking off.

I sat in the H&R coffee shop all morning, reading every word of that Justine Gray person's crappy article, and grew more and more jealous of Arno, with all his connections and the life that he was now assured. The life that, when I woke up this morning, I was sure was mine.

When there were no more words to read, I looked at the pictures. There was Arno in a club, and Arno in his parents' living room with the huge Rothko in the background. Arno on the corner hailing a cab and looking very brooding, with a cigarette dangling from his mouth (and the dude doesn't even smoke). Then there were Rob and David, partying with him in various clubs and some kids' houses that I recognized. They looked like three of a kind, and for a minute I was almost more sad at the way our crew was drifting than the fact that Arno had been named Hottest Private School Boy instead of me.

Then I started looking at the pictures of David, and he wasn't the David that I knew. At least, there was something different about him. He didn't look like the slightly awkward, super tall basketball player I'd always known. He looked almost *cool*.

Was I jealous of David? That was weird. And weirder still: Was David cooler than me now? And then I remembered that he was the only one of my guys I hadn't invited to the party tonight. Instead of wondering what was up with that—and it *was* pretty weird that I would exclude David in any way—I started remembering something else:

I was having a party that night, in honor of being named the Hottest Private School Boy, which of course hadn't happened. I was going to have to get busy, and fast, if I was going to cover up the fact that I'd thought it was going to be me, and not one of my best friends, being celebrated.

arno had no idea he could be
any hotter than he already was

The phone was ringing.

Arno sat up, and after a moment realized that he was himself, in his own bed, and that the weekend was definitely over. The phone was still ringing, too.

"Talk to me," he said, jerking the phone off its charger and sinking back into his pillows.

"Arno? Arno *Wildenburger*?"

"Ye-es?" Arno was not in the mood for guessing games. The voice on the other line giggled rapturously, and then Arno knew who it was. "Mimi? I didn't know you got up this early."

"Only on special occasions. But today *is* kind of a special occasion."

"Oh yeah?" Arno had no idea what she was talking about, but it seemed to bode well for him.

"Uh-huh. I just wanted to be the first to congratulate you. And tell you that you look incredibly hot on the *Hottest Private School Boy* cover."

"Whoa, is that out already?"

"Yes, it is, hot stuff."

Why do some girls think it's cool to be all sugary like that? This was a thought that Arno had, and then forgot very quickly. "Thanks for telling me. What have you got going on this week?"

"Oh, the usual. I think Eugenie Danner is having a party tonight, and there's some other parties tomorrow. Oh, and I guess everyone has started going to Wednesdays at Marquee these days. Why, do you want to hook up?"

"Yeah," Arno said. He was examining his shoulder definition in the mirror now and hadn't really been listening. "Will you call me?"

"Sure thing."

"And Mimi?" he said, remembering how she looked in that befuddlingly low-cut dress, "You looked amazing the other night."

Arno hung up and dialed Rob.

"Santana," he said when the ringing stopped and a groggy voice began making nonsensical noises at the other end of the line.

"Ees eet juh, Vildenbuhgah?" Rob said, and burst out laughing. Arno wasn't sure if it was his new status as HPSB or what, but his patience level was definitely low.

"Cut that dumb-ass shit," Arno said, "and meet me at the Grey Dog Coffee Shop in forty-five, okay?"

He hung up, showered, dressed, and called David to tell him there would be no school today. David protested initially, but there was no saying no to Arno this morning. He was on a roll.

In the foyer, he found a small collection of things for him: a note from his father, on his ecru personal stationery note cards, congratulating Arno and asking if he would like to have a family dinner at Pastis that night; a hand-delivered stack of issues of *New York,* each with his face on the cover, and a note from Justine Gray that read: "Thanks for the wild night Thursday, and all your hot hot help. Best wishes, J.G."; and a huge bouquet of white chrysanthemums.

Arno flipped through the pages of one of the issues. He thought that the cover photo made him look good, but some of the ones inside made him and his guys look stupid, kind of like the Backstreet Boys or something. Arno told himself, *Whatever, get over it,* and then he wondered who in the world would have sent him flowers.

He picked the note off the bouquet and read it:

"Congratulations on making the cover. Can't wait to see you. Xo Xo Lizzie."

Arno smiled to himself. *Yup,* he thought, *getting chicks just got that much easier.* He still had a grin on his face when the doorbell rang, and he wasn't able to wipe the damn thing off by the time he got to the door and opened it.

There was Mimi's friend Sadie, all wrapped up in a sable coat that the weather definitely didn't call for. Arno was confused for a minute: It had been Mimi he'd been flirting with all Thursday night, right? Mimi Rathbone, in the absurdly low-cut dress? Of course, he'd confused these things before.

"Hi, Arno," Sadie said, letting her coat fall open enough to indicate that she wasn't wearing a whole lot underneath. That cleared Arno's head right up. Luckily, he was still holding his cell phone. He called Rob and told him he was going to be a tiny bit late, and he told him to call David and give him the message, too.

Mickey spent all of Monday at school, just to see what that would be like.

It was sort of a letdown.

When the final bell rang, he ran to his locker to deposit the cumbersome books he had accumulated throughout the day, but when he got there he realized that he didn't know his combination. He was pretty sure he had used it once, back in September, or maybe in October, to store a skateboard or something, and he wondered if it was still in there and how he would ever get it out.

There was a note on the door, though.

Mickey picked it up and ripped it open. It was pink, with a red rose design on it, and it looked sort of like a Valentine's card or something. Mickey wasn't usually all that cognizant of dates and major holidays, but he knew that Valentine's Day had already passed. He knew because he and Philippa had gone to Bao 111 for a romantic dinner, and they had gotten into a fight about something. It had been quite a scene, and not only Mickey but all Pardos were now banned from Bao 111. That had caused an even bigger scene.

The card proved to be un-Valentine's-Day-related. It just told him to be at French Roast on Broadway as soon as possible. Both the card and the location were what Mickey's mother would call middlebrow; they certainly weren't things that Philippa would have picked out.

But Mickey was in a mood (he was usually in a mood of some sort), and he set off for French Roast a little buzzed by the mystery. He waved at a few of the kids who were hanging around on the steps of Adele Biggs, but no one really noticed. It was a school full of rich kids who had blown it at other schools, and while they were all very "nurtured," none of them were with it, exactly.

At French Roast, the hostess called him by name and led him to a private table. There were two bowls of hot chocolate on the table, and Philippa was sitting behind one of them.

"I hope this isn't your way of apologizing for the MoMA party, because it really isn't going to cut it," she said. She was holding up a pink card in her small hand. It was identical to the one Mickey had found on his locker.

"When have I ever bought anything pink?" Mickey asked, sitting down and drinking up the hot chocolate. "Or a card, come to think of it. And why didn't you call me back this weekend? I've been going crazy."

"Oh, yeah, I almost forgot. Thanks for freaking my parents out. So why are we here, if you didn't arrange it?" she asked, adding, "Those hot chocolates were here when I got here, you know."

"Maybe someone's trying to kill us," Mickey said. He thought that would be pretty romantic.

Philippa rolled her eyes. "Well, I've got homework," she said, signaling for the waitress, who came over and dropped a silver tray on their table. Instead of a bill, there was another pink card. It instructed them to go to the Excelsior Hotel on West 81st street.

Philippa kept her arms crossed over her chest as they walked down Broadway.

"This had better not be some sort of romantic surprise," Philippa said. "I am *not* getting in trouble for staying in a hotel room with you at this point in my life."

"Phil, how many times do I have to tell you. I didn't arrange this, okay? Would you chill, please?"

She glared at him, but Mickey raised his shades over his eyes, pumped his eyebrows, and gave her the wild-eyed smile that always melted her, at least a little bit. And it did. She almost smiled.

"C'*mon*," Mickey continued. "Just think of this as a treasure hunt or something."

When they walked through the brass revolving doors

of the Excelsior, the concierge approached them and addressed them by name. "You'll want to hurry on up to the tenth floor," he said, before ushering them into the old fashioned elevator. "Room ten E!" he called as the door closed.

Mickey loved surprises, and he was almost having fun. He thought Philippa might feel that way, too. He didn't know what the hell was going on, but it had been a long time since Philippa and he had had an adventure, and it felt good. When they got to 10E, they saw that the door was open. They stepped into a waiting room, which had a few chairs and lots of magazines. There were two doors, both of them closed, one with a pink note on the door. Mickey peeked into the other one.

"Bathroom," he hissed. Philippa giggled.

Mickey went to the other door, and plucked the pink note.

"It says we should come in," he whispered.

"Should we?" she asked.

"Yes," said Mickey. "But whatever happens, I just want you to know that I love you."

"Aw!" said Philippa. She kissed Mickey, and for a moment he re-remembered how warm and sweet she was.

Then she opened the door, and they saw that most frightening of things:

Their parents. Both sets. Together.

They were sitting in big, comfy-looking chairs on either side of a ginormous white desk. Behind the desk was a small man with glasses.

There was a long, awkward moment, and then the man behind the desk said, "I am Dr. Chivers, and this is a relationship intervention."

"A *what*?!" asked Mickey.

"Your parents," said Dr. Chivers, forming a triangle with his fingers, "think that your relationship has perhaps . . . gone too far. We are here to stop it in its tracks and make it right, or say good-bye to it forever. We call it . . . an intervention."

Above the little man with the glasses were large framed posters of hearts. In fact, the whole office was in the color scheme of the Valentine's-esque cards that he and Philippa had received.

"You got that, *mijo*?" Mickey's mother said. She was tapping her long fingernails against the white desk and arching a dramatic black eyebrow.

Mrs. Frady, who was the biggest pushover of the group, tried to smile reassuringly at the couple. "We've all been seeing Dr. Chivers, and it's just done wonders for our marriages," she said. "Not all four of us at once, of course," she added hastily.

"Gross," Mickey said aloud. As usual, he had been unable to stop himself.

"You see, you are going to listen to us tell you about how this relationship has wounded yourselves and the people who love you . . . ," Dr. Chivers said. "And when the intervention portion of your treatment is over, we will begin twice-weekly and—when I deem you ready—weekly sessions to see what we can do to fix the union."

"And if you aren't up to it," said Mr. Frady, who had pretty much always had it in for Mickey and was most definitely not a pushover, "it's real simple: You can stop seeing each other *right now.*"

Mickey's usual feeling that the world and the people that filled it sucked and had to be stopped had just been confirmed about two thousand times over. He looked over at Philippa so they could share this hugely lame moment.

Her face was contorted with disgust. And when she met Mickey's gaze, it looked like she maybe didn't think this relationship was worth the humiliation.

Eight hours later, I was still more or less in a state of shock.

For those of you who have inexplicably forgotten, my crew of guys was falling apart, Arno was named Hottest Private School Boy by *New York* magazine, and I had to make a party that was *supposed* to be for me look like a party for Arno.

Around four, when I had read every word of the Hottest Private School Boy issue about four times over, I decided it was time to get into host mode. I left H&R and went back to my apartment.

Along the way, I called Mickey. I wanted to see if he was coming to the party tonight—in fact, I wanted to be sure of it. The phone rang three times, and then Mickey picked up and said some loud garbled word that sounded like a combination of "Hello" and "What the fuck."

"Hi, Mickey," I said.

"Jonathan?" he said my name sort of desperately, like we hadn't seen each other in twenty years.

"Hey, man I just . . . ," I started to say. Then I think I heard someone in the background going, "No cell phones allowed during intervention." That sounded pretty weird, so I stopped saying what I was saying. Then Mickey told me he had to go.

If I wasn't feeling so sorry for myself, I would have been worried about Mickey. But I was feeling sorry for myself, and worrying about Mickey is a losing game. So I figured I could count Mickey out for tonight.

I stopped in at the market and got the makings for caipirinhas. Maybe I could pull that off as a nod to Arno's Brazilian heritage. Plus, caipirinhas were, or at least had been until recently, one of those hot drinks, so it made sense.

My mom was going to be out for the evening, so I turned down the lights in the living room and put the new Doves album on. I made a practice run of drinks, which required a lot of crushing of lime and sugar. Then I took my practice drink and went and sat in the living room to read *New York* and wonder if anyone would even come, and if they did, how I was going to cover up the fact that all this time I'd been imagining a party for me.

I was almost surprised when I heard Flan "Yoo-hoo" as she opened the door. Then she came in looking—and I know this sounds cheesy—like an angel. She was wearing boxy chino shorts that made her legs look even more long and girlish, and a red-and-white-striped Petit Bateau shirt that showed off her long neck, and high-heeled jellies.

"How was school?" I asked.

She shrugged and sat down next to me. "I have a lot of homework this week. It kinda sucks, I guess," she said. She seemed a little glum. "And I had a fight with Daria today. She was mad that I was ditching the sleepover."

"That's too bad. Did you see this?" I asked, handing her the *New York,* which had come out of the bookstore with me, in my back pocket. Who would pay good money for lies like that? Although I did feel a little bad because I'd never shoplifted before.

Flan made a noise like *mmm-hmmm.* She didn't seem appropriately shocked to me, but I was probably being sensitive.

"But can you believe that Arno was the one they wanted?"

"Yeah, that's weird," Flan said unconvincingly.

"Weird is one way of putting it. Perverse might be another."

"So, who's coming tonight?" she asked.

"I dunno, probably nobody," I said.

"No, I'm sure people will come," Flan said sweetly.

"I'd actually rather be alone at this particular moment in time. But if people do come, can we just pretend that the party was for Arno being named HPSB all along? It's all kind of . . . you know . . . embarrassing."

To my relief, people did come. And they all seemed to be under the impression that they'd been coming to Arno's party all along, so it wasn't too hard to fake it. Pretty soon my relief mutated into irritation, though—I mean, why would they just assume that? The first thing out of everyone's mouth was, "This is *so* exciting. How long have you known about Arno being HPSB?"

I also realized that being a host isn't always fun. I had to keep running back and forth to the kitchen to make people more drinks. Apparently, the caipirinha is still very popular.

When Arno arrived, there were about twenty-five kids hanging out in my living room talking about him. David and Rob were close behind, with those three Florence girls they had been partying with at the MoMA party. They all looked very cool, and like they'd been having maximum fun.

I went over to greet them.

"Thanks for throwing me a party," Arno said, even though I'd never told him that the party was for him. He looked more tanned and well taken care of already, and he surveyed the room as if to say "Not half bad." He was wearing a motorcycle jacket that I'd never seen him wear before, too. Then he leaned over and whispered, "And thanks for getting us on the list at Lotus; I think that really impressed the *New York* girl. I talked us into the VIP room later, too. It was pretty sweet."

"Sounds like good times," I said.

"Totally. And then later I started DJ-ing. I mean, that was hot."

"How did you pull that one off?" I asked, going more for incredulous than jealous.

"Oh, you know, my friend Billy DJs there," Arno continued. "I just told him I was trying to make a good impression. He was all about it."

"You let me know next time you throw party," Rob interrupted, throwing his arm around my neck. "I could have helped! I love to party."

"I know," I said. Then I looked at their girls, who were a little overdressed, like they were going to a nightclub or something. "Can I get you ladies caipirinhas?"

"I *love* caipirinhas," one of the girls said. It was Mimi Rathbone.

I walked them into the living room, and everyone gasped when they saw Arno. I said, "Boys and girls, this guy just wandered in off the street. Apparently, he's a teeny-weeny bit hot. Will you entertain him while I make another round of drinks?"

Everyone laughed and then started loudly admiring Arno. Let it be noted that the best way to hide your jealousy is to be fake mean. Everyone assumes you're being cute and self-effacing, when in fact you mean every word. I slipped back into the kitchen, relieved that I had six caipirinhas to muddle.

I kept a forced smile on my face, and did a good job pretending like I thought it was awesome that Arno had been named Hottest Private School Boy the whole time he was there, but it was probably a good thing that, after only forty-five minutes, he said he would have to be leaving pretty soon. I really couldn't have kept it up much longer.

"At least have another round of drinks, man," I said. Mimi Rathbone and her friend Lizzie were dancing in the middle of the living room now. It was almost like they'd brought the nightclub with them.

"Okay," Arno said. Then he lowered his voice, and added, "You should get rid of these people and go to Ginger with us."

I was about to say that, yeah, I'd been wanting to go to Ginger for a while now, when I remembered about Flan. I hadn't had a chance to talk to her all night, what with all my schmoozing, and now I didn't even know where she was. I was definitely going to be in trouble if I ditched the party. She had, after all, canceled her girls' night for me. It took everything I had to say, "Nah, I've heard that place is a little much."

"Suit yourself."

"I will," I said as I went back into the kitchen.

But a funny thing happened, as I stood there crushing limes and sugar for the next round of drinks. I heard two people whispering urgently in the hall. And one of them was Flan. She was saying:

"Are you here with Mimi Rathbone and her friends?"

"Um, yeah, but it's really not what it looks like. . . ."

"Because there's something I have to tell you. . . ."

She sounded almost angry. Before I could stop myself, I said, "Flan!?" and peeped around the corner.

There she was, looking surprised. And guilty. David was standing next to her.

"What are you talking about?" I said.

"Nothing," Flan said. Then the buzzer went off, and she said, "I think that's Patch. He just called. I better go get it," and disappeared.

David and I stared at each other awkwardly for a minute. What kind of secret would Flan share with David? And why did she look so guilty when she saw me?

"Well, uh, I think we're going soon," David said lamely.

I couldn't believe he got to go to Ginger and hang out with Danny Abraham and probably meet celebrities and get photographed and written about. And then I realized that if David was cooler than I was now, maybe Flan would like him more than me. There was just something not right about that little scene, them whispering out in the hall.

David interrupted my jealous train of thought by saying, "But, um, thanks for the party. I mean, you never actually told me about it, but . . . Anyway, it seems like a while since we've—"

"Yeah, whatever," I said, thrusting the caipirinha I'd been carrying into his hand. I wasn't sure exactly what was going on, but it made me all sick-feeling inside. "You better drink this up, and then get out of my apartment as fast as you can."

This was supposed to be It, and David knew that.

He, Arno, Rob, and the It Girls glided on down the Avenue (Tenth, he was pretty sure), past the line of people yelling and scrambling and, worst of all, waiting behind the velvet rope. They walked right on past them and into where the lights were low and the girls were flashy and the music was loud.

Really, really loud. (Pumping? Was he supposed to say that the music was "pumping"? Or was that word over already?)

Their group pushed into the crowd, which caused a ripple of excitement through the club. David had never been to this one before, but Arno had said it was called Ginger and that it was crucial for them to hit this spot because he had made a personal promise to the owner or something. Everyone was shouting hello to Arno and congratulating him, and it seemed like a lot of the girls were trying to touch him. A chant of "HPSB" came up from the dance floor, and the people on the mezzanine all stopped what they were doing and looked down on Arno and his guys.

They were It, and they were cruising with It Girls. But David could hardly think straight, the music was so loud. He sort of wished they could turn it down a little bit.

And David probably would have benefited from some straight thinking right then, because he was confused about many things. For instance, it was weird that everybody already knew about this Hottest Private School Boy thing. David lived a life pretty circumscribed by basketball and didn't have much time for extracurricular reading, but still, the issue had come out that *morning*. How did all these people already know that Arno was HPSB? He was also confused about why a drink in this kind of place cost precisely twice what it cost anywhere else. (Not that that was such a big concern; nobody had asked them to pay at the door, and it was looking like no one was going to ask them to pay for anything else, either.)

David was also confused about what had just happened at Jonathan's apartment. What had Flan wanted to tell him? And why had Jonathan been so short with him?

The hostess led them to the VIP area and sat them in a booth. She was pretty, in the same way the It Girls were pretty. She had long, straight blond hair with shiny skin two shades darker than her hair. It was beginning to seem a little bit strange to David that all the girls in his life now seemed so plastic and identical. He wasn't even sure how anyone kept the It Girls' names straight. He had already confused them twice that night. Plus, David couldn't help comparing every girl to the one he'd met at the MoMA, the one who could have been Modigliani's muse. She was so . . . *different*. He couldn't help looking to see if she was at the club, even though he knew he was supposed to be into the blonde who was sitting next to him.

"This is *so* embarrassing . . . but would you sign my issue?" the hostess asked Arno, handing the magazine to him. He gave her a little nod of acknowledgment, and scrawled his name on the cover. She hugged it to herself like a teddy bear. "Thanks so much. Danny said everything's on the house tonight, so drink up!"

The girls all made little noises of approval, and Arno looked out at the scene like it was pretty everyday to him. Which was actually true.

When the hostess was gone, Mimi leaned into Arno and nibbled his ear. She said, "You know I *love* Ginger."

"It's hot," said Lizzie.

"Okay, I'm going to pee," Mimi said. She looked at Arno and added: "Who's coming?"

"I'll go," said Sadie.

"I'll stay," said Lizzie. Mimi shot her a look. When the other girls were gone, Lizzie leaned in and nibbled Arno's other ear.

David stood up to look around for the Modigliani again. He got good range because he was so tall, but still, all he could see were girls with heavily made-up faces and newsboy caps. When he sat back down, he noticed that Arno and Lizzie were making out. Wasn't Arno just with the other one? David really *was* going crazy. A cocktail waitress brought them a bottle of Grey Goose and mixers. She asked Arno to sign her HPSB issue as well. Then Rob came and joined them; David hadn't even noticed that he was gone.

"Yeah, wild tonight!" Rob said loudly and to no one in particular as he slid into the booth. Lizzie moved away from Arno quickly, but Rob didn't seem to notice what had been going on. He poured them all drinks. "To cool girls and hot boys!" he said as he lifted his vodka cran. David was relieved when he noticed Arno cringe, just a little bit, at that.

They all focused on their drinks for a moment, and looked out at the crowd. The people were really packed in, and everyone was getting down, their drinks flowing over, and trying to shout over the music, which was futile. Rob told them all to look when P. Diddy came in, with a herd of bodyguards surrounding him. Then Mimi and Sadie came back.

"We miss anything?" Mimi said, glaring at Lizzie.

"Not much," said Lizzie.

"Fine. Let's dance, bitch," said Mimi. The three of them went to the dance floor, and started dancing in a row. They were all really close, and they closed their eyes and appeared to be really feeling the music. David thought they looked like they knew what they were doing.

"Del *fuego*!" said Rob.

"Yeah, they're hot pieces," Arno said, looking briefly around the club. People seemed to be looking at him, too.

Rob looked back at David and Arno. Gone was the stupid party face he wore virtually all the time. He looked serious. He looked like he had been thinking.

"I have something we must discuss," he said. Then he looked up and saw the girls coming back from the dance floor. The goofy face reappeared. "But first . . ."

Mimi leaned over toward Arno in a way that seemed, to David, somewhat clumsy. But it occurred to him that it also might have been sexy. After all, they could all see down her shirt now.

"You guys weren't paying *any* attention to us," she said, sticking her bottom lip out.

"You know how it is," Arno said.

"Come on!" said Lizzie, beginning to shake to the new Jay-Z song that had just come on.

"Yeah, baby!" Rob yelled in a misguided Austin Powers accent. He stood up, and he and the girls headed for the dance floor, gesturing at Arno to follow.

Arno stood up, ready to follow them. But before he did, he leaned in and hissed at David: "There are three hot girls out there, and we are three hot guys. If you don't stop mooning, we're going to be three girls and two guys, and that's illegal in some states. So start acting normal. Got it?"

Arno was experiencing two different emotions at once.

Everywhere he went—on the street, at Pastis, and now at Ginger—people stared at him. Not the usual, "who is that good looking dude?" stare. It was a longer, more reverential kind of staring, equal parts awe and adoration. People kept giving him things, too, and most of it looked pricey. He felt like the sun. Or like the sun was shining on him. Or something.

But in spite of all this warmth, he felt tense, too. He felt like he had gone from coffee boy to CEO in one day, and the pressure was enormous. Trying to keep David and Rob in line, for instance. David was acting like a real downer recently.

Now that he was at the heart of the club, surrounded by people chanting his name, hearing the really cool, loud music, he was feeling mostly just good. And hot, of course.

"You're so hot," Mimi said. They had been dancing for almost an hour. She gave him a knowing little smile out of the corner of her mouth. She looked almost miniature next to him. But hot, definitely hot.

But that was another thing. Sadie seemed to be acting like nothing had happened that morning, even though they'd fooled around pretty seriously, and Mimi seemed either not to know or not to care. Arno thought they were both hot, but he didn't want to get ambushed by angry girls later on down the road. He really needed David to help him out with this by distracting Sadie.

Arno looked up, and saw Danny Abraham, HPSB '04, in his mezzanine booth, and waved. Danny raised his glass to Arno, and then went back to the three blond girls surrounding him. It was like Arno had been anointed.

Then the new Kelis song came on, and the crowd lifted Mimi and a few other girls up and put them on the bar. They started dancing, and the crowd started screaming and cheering. Arno slipped back to the booth.

Rob was wiping the sweat off his forehead with a hand towel, and David was sitting next to him. He had obviously been sitting there for a while, and he looked a little glum.

Arno did an obligatory round of waving and "what's up" chin motioning to his admirers, and then leaned back in the booth. Rob poured him a drink, which was cold and good. Then Rob said, in a tone lower than he

95

had ever used before, "I have been discussing with Chino."

"Who's Chino?" said Arno. He checked out the girls, who were still dancing on the bar.

"The doorman of Ginger, where we are," said Rob. "You know, the one who let us in. And he no charge us. So nice!"

"Yeah, well his boss told him not to," said Arno with a shrug.

"Yes, the boss very nice, too. But what we discuss is this: you know how much they charge for a door here?"

"They sell doors here?" David said. He had been staring glassily out at the crowd and was snapped back into the conversation by Rob's illogical statement.

"Davey, pay attention," Arno said. He snapped his fingers, which was probably what his father would have done. "He's talking about the door charge. What's wrong with you?"

"Oh," said David.

"Guess! Guess the door charge!" Rob said.

"Twenty?" said Arno.

"Twenty-five," Rob said with satisfaction. Arno shrugged again. He was feeling very blasé about everything lately.

"That's a lot," said David. He looked away quickly, like he knew that made him sound uncool.

"What's your point?" Arno said. The serious Rob was getting on his nerves.

"Are you thinking what I'm thinking?" Rob said.

Arno shifted in his seat. "That doesn't seem very likely."

"Because what I am thinking," said Rob, "is that this whole room adores you. This city adores you."

Arno nodded. That did seem to be the case.

"If you are Hottest School Boy, why not have Hot School Boy party! And we can charge twenty dollars at the door." Rob rubbed his palms together. Then he quickly added: "Because that is what it will take to throw a party hot enough for Arno."

"That's an idea," Arno said. He saw Mimi coming from the dance floor. Her skin had a sheen to it from the dancing, and she looked incredibly ripe and gorgeous. She was making the beckoning motion that women in beer commercials frequently make. "I'll consider it," he said absentmindedly, standing up, and walking toward Mimi.

Then he had a thought. He turned back to Rob, who was obviously still thinking about his party planning, and David, who was obviously still not fun.

"In the meantime, would you do me a favor, Rob? Figure out what to do with this old man."

When they got outside, it occurred to David that Rob had gone a record length of time without a cigarette. He was smoking now, though, and talking with Chino the doorman. He was making precise little motions with his hands like he was getting exact details. David waited for him against the wall, a little bit farther down the block.

Chino got busy with the door again, and Rob lit another cigarette and sauntered over to David.

"Those girls are crazy," Rob said. David realized that he should probably teach Rob a few adjectives besides *wild, crazy,* and *hot.* At least, if he wanted to keep hanging out with Rob and not go insane he should. "They make Arno sandwich!"

Before Rob had escorted him out, Mimi, Lizzie, and Sadie had all started dancing with Arno in the middle of the dance floor. It had caused a lot of excitement in the club, but it wasn't really a sandwich, at least not David's definition of a sandwich.

To David, the word "sandwich" implied a kind of

grade school snack time innocence, while what had been going on inside the club had seemed increasingly . . . dirty.

"It's late," said David with a sigh. What he wanted to say was, "Can we please go now?"

"I think Arno's unpleased with you," Rob said. He clicked his tongue in disapproval. "It's because you are so downer like that. Who cares if it is late, whatever that means, anyway. We should be like vampires, and know the city only when it is late."

"What?" said David. He had heard the word "vampire," which he didn't like at all.

"Tell me why. Why you don't like those crazy, sexy girls?" Rob asked, making a pouting face.

David made the brave decision, and tried to be honest. "I don't know . . . ," he said. "They seem a little plastic."

"Yes," Rob said, nodding emphatically. "The plastic surgery is excellent on them."

"Oh," David said. That was pretty baffling. And yet, so fitting.

"So . . . what's *el problemo*?"

"I just think that Sadie might not be my type, exactly," David said. He said it slower than he meant to, but Rob still looked like he was having trouble chewing on that one.

"Mmmmm . . . you don't feel love for Sadie?" Rob said. In fact, he was talking pretty slow as well.

"No," David said. For the first time that night, he felt like laughing, "I don't feel love for her."

"And you have a, how you say, different type?"

David nodded. "I think so. . . ."

"I knew it!" Rob said.

"You did?" David asked. He was surprised, but also a little relieved. Maybe someone did understand him.

"You feel love for another girl!"

"Well, love, that's a big word. . . ."

"It is hard to tell sometime." Was this romance advice from *Rob*? "She is very beautiful, in a different way."

"I know." David was actually smiling now. "But I think that's why I like her. She's different, you know?"

"Yes! I get her back for you!"

"Back?" David was confused again. Rob looked like he was about to do a merry little dance.

"Yes, we get Flan back for you!"

"Flan?" David's mouth hung open. "No, I—"

"David, don't be shy. I have many powers. . . ."

"I know, it's just that Flan's not—"

Rob held his hand up. "I know, she's not single. And Jonathan is your friend. But he's also not really, am I right?"

David paused. Jonathan *had* been pretty weird and

mean at his party. Which he hadn't even invited David to, which was also pretty weird and mean.

"And Flan, she is lovely, is she not?"

David nodded. He wished he hadn't had those three vodka crans back there. His head was sort of swimming, and Rob was confusing. From now on, he was definitely a beer-only kind of guy.

"Rob, the thing is . . . ," David said.

"No buts!" said Rob.

"What?"

"David, I'm making this my number one priority, right after the Hot School Boy party. Flan will be yours again!"

The sky was starting to turn purple, and tomorrow was Tuesday. It was a quarter past three in the morning, and school would be starting in a few hours. That was when David stopped trying to convince Rob that he didn't want to steal Flan away from Jonathan.

Because right then, thinking about the way Jonathan had completely abandoned him, and how he'd asked David to leave his house that night . . . well, David felt like that might be just what Jonathan deserved.

If Philippa didn't have to go through with it, too, Wednesday would definitely have been the worst day of Mickey's life—a life that included several emergency room visits, and a whole lot of time when he was grounded. Boredom, to Mickey, was more painful than pain, and where he had to be Wednesday afternoon was definitely going to be boring.

He'd spent all morning dreading it, and could hardly concentrate at school, which he had been attending reliably all week because his parents were on a crackdown. When he got out of school, he saw Caselli, the dude who ran his dad's studio, waiting for him.

"Ready for therapy?" he asked. Caselli was also Mickey's unofficial guardian. He was wearing the white coveralls worn by all of Ricardo Pardo's assistants, and his head had been recently shaved. He looked like Mickey's older, cleaner brother.

"Yeah, I'd rather be torn apart by sharks." Mickey paused. "Actually, that sounds kind of cool. . . . But seriously, man—you really didn't have to escort me. I wouldn't make Philippa go through this alone."

"Dad's orders," Caselli said, smiling only a little bit. "Get on."

Mickey climbed on the back of Caselli's vintage Triumph. It hurt him to be a passenger, and not the runaway driver of the motorcycle, but at least the ride was something exciting on the way to Dr. Chivers's office.

Philippa was already there when he walked in. She was looking unusually tiny and Goth today, wearing an oversized mohair sweater, which she had belted at the waist, over a long black skirt. Her straight brown hair was parted down the middle, falling below her shoulders, and her lips were painted a deep red. She was also glaring at him.

"Welcome to couples' counseling, Mickey," Dr. Chivers said. He had a kind of brittle, ingratiating smile that made Mickey feel uncomfortable. He was wearing a red shirt, pink tie, and mocha suit jacket. This also made Mickey uncomfortable. Dr. Chivers waved to the armchair next to Philippa's and said, "Please have a seat."

Mickey leaned over to kiss Philippa on the cheek. She jerked her head away from him.

"Let's begin with that," Dr. Chivers said. "My

methodology is: Start small, and grow the concept of your relationship, so that we can understand it as never before. So, Mickey, why do you think Philippa pulled away from you like that?"

"Because she's pissed she has to spend her afternoon talking about feelings . . . ?" Mickey said as neutrally as possible.

"Mickey, could you shut up please so that we can just get this over with?" Philippa snapped.

"What'd I say?"

Philippa rolled her eyes, and Mickey sunk back into his chair.

"Okay," said Dr. Chivers, "that might not be the best approach for you two. We could try a method that involves a special, malleable clay of my own design. You play with it and just see what flows out of you. You'd be amazed at how your subconscious reveals itself in the clay's form."

Philippa and Mickey stared at him in silence.

"It has been remarkably effective with both sets of your parents," he offered.

"No!" Mickey and Philippa shouted instinctively.

"Well, what do you say we go simple, then?"

"That would be best," Philippa said.

"Whatever," Mickey muttered.

"So . . . why do you think this relationship is so

plagued by fighting and betrayal? What is rotten in this union? Mickey?"

"Dude," Mickey said. He tried to calm his voice, but only a little bit. "Nothing's rotten. Like, I'm an intense motherfucker, you know? We're *intense*. That ain't rotten."

"That's an interesting interpretation. Philippa?"

Philippa shifted in her chair uncomfortably. She looked at Mickey, whose eyes were blazing in her direction, full of the hope that she would say to hell with this, and ask him to elope or something equally wild and intense. "I think the problem with our relationship is that I'm gay," she said calmly. Then she put her face in her hands.

Mickey made a cackling noise. God he loved her! Philippa was definitely the only girl who could keep up with his games.

Dr. Chivers clapped his hands together in irritation. "Now, Philippa, many people deal with the discomfort of discussing their feelings by lying and employing the tone popularly referred to as sarcasm in our modern culture. But that's really not what this place—and this practice—is all about. So please, if you want to continue, check your games at the door. Mickey and I know perfectly well that you are not a lesbian." When he said "lesbian" he made quotation marks with his fingers, which seemed odd to Mickey. "Would you like to try again?"

Philippa made an exasperated noise. She looked up at the ceiling and seemed to be thinking. She examined her cuticles, uncrossed and recrossed her legs, and sighed. Then, in a voice that sounded both tired and very, very old, she said, "Well, Mickey and I have been going out since freshman year, and that's a pretty long time. At first, it was really wild and fun, and we just surprised each other all the time. But the shit Mickey does now doesn't surprise me anymore, you know what I mean? I just think the days when we excite each other might be . . . over."

Mickey wasn't sure how the rest of the hour passed, or how he got home. But for the rest of the night all he could think about was the fact that he wasn't exciting anymore, even to his girlfriend. *Especially* to his girlfriend. It was not a fun feeling. It was the opposite of fun.

He looked so bummed at dinner that his parents didn't even yell at him much.

"How was therapy, *mijo*?" Lucy Pardo asked. She was a gorgeous ex-model, and Mickey got all of his good looks from her. When she was in the right mood, she thought Mickey was the most amazing thing to have happened in the history of man.

Mickey shrugged.

"How was school?"

"Whatever," Mickey said. "Will you pass the empanadas?"

Ricardo passed him a platter covered with a dishcloth. "The reviews of the Vogel show have started to come out," he said. "I didn't really think it was all *that* bad."

Mickey looked up at his dad. That was *it*.

He ran out of the slightly decayed formal dining room, down the hall, and into the library. The Pardos kept all their art books there, as well as bound copies of all the little art journals that Ricardo read obsessively for mentions of his work.

Mickey found the Vs (one of Ricardo's assistants had the weekly task of alphabetizing their collection), and pulled out the Luc Vogel monograph. He flipped through the pages, from one naked scene to another. Vogel had been right: not a restaurant in the bunch.

Mickey thought about how bummed Luc Vogel had been at the opening, and that cheered him up a little bit. That guy was an artist, and he'd been making sure that his career meant taking life to the maximum for years. *He* was exciting, and he could still feel low. Then Mickey remembered the dare.

That's when Mickey knew what he had to do to make

himself exciting again. He knew what he had to do to get Philippa back for real. He was going to take that dare. He was going to stuff a restaurant full of naked people, and he was going to photograph every minute of it.

i get jealous about something way important

My world was still pretty dark and cruel-feeling midweek, and on Wednesday, when I got home from school, I had the unpleasant surprise of finding Rob in my room. He was wearing a royal blue robe with gold piping that had been my dad's in the eighties, and his feet were up on my desk.

I realized that I hadn't seen him since my party, which was when I saw something weird happening between Flan and David, which had been unsettling my mind ever since. I sort of knew I'd blown it out of proportion when I'd asked David to leave, but also I kind of felt like all those guys had it coming for thinking they were so cool. Now, seeing Rob didn't make me feel any better. It just reminded me that he—and David—were in the Hottest Private School Boy club, and I was not. They must have been out doing fabulous things all week.

"Hey, Rob, it's cool that you stay at the apartment now," I said, even though it actually wasn't. "But this is still my room. Okay?"

Rob looked at me like I had suggested he get off my island—which actually would have been quite pleasant—and it looked like he took my comment pretty hard.

"Well I'm sorry, Jon, I only needed a surface to work on my scrapbook, and there is no desk in my room."

Scrapbook? I was ready just to pick up the whole mess and hurl it out the window, but the sad look on Rob's face stopped me. I went over to have a charitable look at the many snapshots that Rob had laid out on my nice, clean desk. This seemed to make him happy, and then something occurred to me. Maybe Rob, for all his bravado and all the weird ways he can smell, was giving me a clue about something.

"Want to see?" he asked. He was smiling now. And was that niceness in his voice? It sounded like nice. "You recognize some of these characters, no?"

And I did. There was Rob, in the Floods' house, making out with February. (Not so pleasant.) And there were Feb and Flan, sitting at the big butcher block table in the Floods' kitchen, drinking wine.

Same picture, plus David. The pictures kept going like that, with David getting closer and closer to Flan like a horrible flip book: David moving stiltedly across the room, Flan sitting on his lap, everyone lifting their wineglasses. Cheers! Then her arms around his neck, then kissing his cheek. Feb making a "Gross!" face at the camera.

Some of the color must have drained from my face, because Rob said—still sounding like he cared, a lot—"Are you fine?"

No, I really wasn't. David was in the HPSB elite crew now. He could probably have any girl he wanted, so why not take Flan? He'd obviously almost had her already while I was away.

I was going to lose my girl, I could feel it, and that really was not fine with me.

"Jonathan, does this bother you? I know you and Flan are together now, and I'm sure you wonder what happened between David and her over last winter."

I shook my head, too vehemently, and said, too quickly, "Not really."

"Because it would worry me, too. But nothing happened!"

I felt my shoulders relax a bit, but then Rob added:

"They were just insanely attracted to each other, that is all."

My impulse was to run, but here was Rob, and he was giving me information. Information I really needed. "Do you think he—they—might . . . again?" I said.

Rob looked left and right, as though someone might be listening in on our conversation. Which was ridiculous, of course. My mom had had all the walls reinforced three years ago, so she wouldn't have to listen to my brother and me playing loud music, not to mention that she wouldn't care about this chat—not at all.

"Jonathan, I really shouldn't say . . ."

I nodded. Of course he wasn't going to say. He was David's friend, after all. "I gotta go," I said, moving to the door. "To meet Flan. Take as long as you want, really."

I backed into the door, and reached for the knob. What was that look he was giving me? Was it guilt? He said: "But be careful of your feelings, brother Jon, I don't want you to get hurt."

When I got to the Floods' place, I tried to call Flan, but she didn't pick up. I went up to her room, but she wasn't there, so I wandered out to the backyard, where I found Patch cooking tuna steaks.

It was a lovely twilight time of day, and that nice smoky cooking smell filled the backyard.

"Hey, man," he said. He reached his hand out for a behind the back high five. "You hungry?"

"Um, Patch? What are you doing?" None of my guys cook, unless making sandwiches or dialing Odeon counts. The Wildenburgers, Pardos, and Floods (at least when they're in Connecticut) all have personal cooks; the Grobarts have Zabars deliver prepared foods to their apartment four times a week, and my mom has Zone meals come to our place three times a day and lets me order in whatever I want.

"Cooking." Patch flipped one of the pieces of fish. "There's rice and soy-lime marinade, too," he added.

"But *why* are you cooking?" I took a can of Asahi from the six-pack sitting on the picnic table.

Patch seemed to be seriously considering my question for a minute. "I guess I wanted to try something new. My parents were supposed to be coming down from the country today, but they canceled. And Flan had to stay at school for an algebra study session because she has a test

113

tomorrow. February is upstairs. Maybe she'll want some. But there's plenty for you."

"Actually, I'm going over to Freeman's a little later. With Flan, I think. Hey, are you okay?"

There was definitely something weird going on with Patch. I took a sip of the beer and wondered what it could be, and also why Flan hadn't told me that she had a test to study for. Maybe David was skipping basketball practice. . . . I wondered if she was really still at school.

"I guess I'm having one of those moments where I don't really know why I should be excited about life, you know?" Patch flipped another piece of fish, and then the other three. He cracked a can of Asahi, too. "Like, I feel like I'm always looking for something to want and need, but nothing can really hold my attention that long. I was thinking today how, when we were in the Mediterranean, everything was cool, know what I mean? Just hanging out with you guys and Greta. And it made me want seafood."

Greta was this girl Patch hooked up with on that cruise ship. I think he really liked her, but she lives in California.

I am not proud of what I did next. But Patch is not a needy guy. Things are easy for him, and I have just never known him to be depressed. But I was pretty depressed right then, too, so I did what I had to. I changed the subject back to me:

"Hey, does Flan really have a test tomorrow?"

"Yeah, why?"

"I just feel bad I didn't know," I lied.

"Anyway," Patch said, giving me a weird look, "I just keep doing new things and it all seems old already." He lifted the tuna steaks off the grill and put them onto a big dish. Then he put two of them on plates, drizzled marinade across them, and gave each a clump of rice. "Just try this, okay?" He handed me one of the plates, and sat down. Then he continued, "I'm just trying to figure out what it's all about, you know?"

I took a bite of the fish, and to my total surprise, it was really good. Shockingly, celebrity-chef good. "Maybe you should start a restaurant?"

"Nah, cooking's boring. I mean, how do people get so excited about something you have to do three times a day for the rest of your life? It sucks." Patch sighed.

"Yeah, I don't get people," I said. "I mean, do you understand how Arno could be chosen for Hottest Private School Boy? He's so obvious. I mean, that Justine lady told me . . . I mean, it *seemed* like she was telling me that they wanted me. And then . . . the world just doesn't make sense sometimes, you know?"

"Yeah, like that Justine person is so incredibly concerned with stupid shit. It's like everything has to be reduced to little bite-size pieces, and . . ."

I think Patch was just trying to make me feel better. Which was nice, considering he seemed seriously bummed. But I couldn't help being distracted by the idea of Flan and David. After all, they were probably at this very minute meeting in secret in some terribly cool place that only Arno and his entourage could get into. She was probably being very cozy and sweet to him, the way she used to be with me. And why not? I hadn't even been to Ginger, and who knew if I would be able to get us into Freeman's tonight.

Patch was still saying something about that Justine person.

"Do you think some friend of the Wildenburgers' is editor-in-chief at *New York* or something?" I interrupted. "I mean, maybe Justine did pick me, but then they had to change it because of some insider politics."

Patch was shaking his head. "J, it doesn't matter. Can't you see that?"

"But it *does* matter," I said. I couldn't even believe I was saying these things—this was not my usual good friend persona coming through—but I couldn't help it. I just kept hammering away.

"How? Give me one example," Patch said.

"Well . . ." I took a deep breath, and came clean: "I think . . . I think . . . maybe David and Flan are having an affair."

Patch shook his head, this time with a little laugh, but I kept on going. "I know it's not totally related, but now he's friends with Arno, and Arno's hot, so his friends are hot. I just think, maybe David can do more for her at this point than I can, or at least, maybe it seems that way."

"But David isn't *Arno's* friend—we're all *friends*, right? And besides, what would make you think that Flan is interested in David *at all*?"

"I was just talking to Rob, and . . ."

Patch dropped his fork on his plate like I had just said a bad word and like we were people who got offended by bad words. He got very intense all of a sudden, and said, "Listen carefully: Hottest Private School Boy is one big, bad, trumped-up lie. And Rob is, too."

Arno was sitting in front of Café Gitane wearing sunglasses and sipping rosé. Next to him was Mimi, hiding under huge black Prada sunglasses and Arno's white Sean John blazer, which was draped over her shoulders. Even though it was a stunningly warm spring afternoon, she had seemed to really want to wear his jacket.

Since Monday, they had hooked up five times. That was two days ago, so they were getting to know each other pretty fast.

Everyone who walked by them on Mott Street waved and giggled and wondered aloud if that was "really him." A few of the girls put down their big white shopping bags and asked for Arno's autograph. He was loving every minute of it.

"Ah, for a little peace and quiet," Arno said, after a few Florence underclassmen had finally left. He made a big fake yawning noise and stretched his arms over his head.

"I know, baby," she sighed, leaning over and snuggling

him sympathetically. He couldn't be sure, but she seemed not to have gotten that he was kidding.

A car pulled up, and a balding guy in what looked like a safari jacket leaned out of the driver's seat and started snapping pictures of them.

"More paparazzi!" Arno said in disbelief. It was absurd, but kind of funny, too.

"Get lost!" Mimi shrieked. She didn't seem to see the humor in this little episode, either.

"Hey, I'm just an average guy, nothing exciting, right?" Arno said nonchalantly to the guy with the camera. He didn't really think he was an average guy, but it was hotter to shrug off his new celebrity and its encroachment on his privacy than to get all pissy about it, or to act too flattered.

"Come on, Arno!" the guy said, and so Arno mugged good-naturedly for him a few times. The guy thanked him, and then the car pulled away. A few minutes later, Rob and David came walking down the street. David was carrying big shopping bags, and Rob had a huge cheesy smile on his face. They all slapped hands hello, and sat down. Mimi just waved, because by that point she was on her cell phone.

"So what's on for tonight?" Arno asked. David shrugged. "Man, do *not* be a mope. We're going out, right?"

"Sure," David said, "I just bought all new clothes so that I could, you know, feel comfortable in clubs and stuff. So I have to go out for that reason alone."

"How could we not go out? We always go out!" Rob added loudly. "I was thinking we start at Freeman's, you know, keep it downtown. Then Lit maybe? So important you don't lose your downtown cred, so I am thinking we go there."

"Cool," Arno said. He took another sip of his cold pink wine. Mimi ended her call and whispered in Arno's ear that she had to go home and change for tonight. He told her that was cool, too, and she blew into his ear. Then she handed his blazer back.

"I'm going to catch a cab on Houston," she said, and wiggled her fingers at David and Rob. All three of them watched as her shiny exercised legs carried her swiftly up Mott. Mimi did not seem to have a lot of skirts that went below mid-thigh.

"So, you two . . . ?" Rob asked, pumping his eyebrows annoyingly.

"Cut it," Arno said. Why was Rob annoying him so much today?

"She's hot, that's all!" Rob giggled.

"So what did you get?" Arno asked David.

David proudly showed him this orange Perry Ellis blazer and the Diesel jeans he'd gotten, as well as some faded designer T-shirts he'd found at this consignment store called Ina. "Nice, right?"

Arno snorted instinctively, but he was actually glad that David was cooling out a little bit. "Nice choices," he said.

David looked relieved by Arno's approval, and then relieved again that they didn't have to talk fashion anymore; the waitress had appeared at their table. Rob ordered a bottle of "whatever Arno's drinking" and some olives. When she had served them and disappeared again, he put his elbows on the table and clasped his hands. "So . . . have you given any thought to the Hot Boy party?"

Arno popped an olive in his mouth.

"Rob, I'm not sure it's such a hot idea."

"Arno, baby, don't be so brash. Let us celebrate you!"

A group of girls walked by and, bizarrely, did *not* notice Arno. David looked after them in a weird way, like he recognized them but wasn't sure.

"I really don't know if I have time these days. I don't even have time to return my calls, you know what I mean?"

Rob nodded understandingly.

"I mean, this whole Hottest Private School Boy thing is great, don't get me wrong. I wouldn't trade it for the world. But it's a lot of responsibility, too, and you guys

121

can't even get with that." Arno smiled to himself, like he thought of a really good joke. "It's like I'd need an *intern* just to manage my social calendar."

"That's *it*!" Rob exclaimed. "That's what we do! I be your intern. Hottest Private Intern." He put on a very sober face and added, "It would be an honor."

"You're going to be my intern?" Arno asked. Sometimes, it was really hard not to pity Rob—he so obviously didn't get the meaning of Intern. Arno shrugged and said, "Why not. You're hired."

"Bravo! As your intern, my first order of business is getting this party together. It's going to be this Saturday, which is very soon, but luckily I've already started making arrangements. There will be the flyering to do, of course, and the beer . . ."

"Rob. I don't have the time, remember? So I don't even want to know," Arno said, laughing. God, he was in a good mood today. It was like everything was just funny to him. "Don't ask, don't tell, okay?"

"Of course, Jefe." Rob lit a cigarette, and crossed his legs. He looked extremely pleased with himself. David looked up and down the street, like he didn't quite know where he fit in to all this.

Across the street, a group of girls who went to Potterton were pointing and gasping at Arno. One of them looked like she was about to faint.

"Duty calls," Arno said. He loosened his shoulders, stood up, and strode across the street to sign the girls' T-shirts.

David still looked distracted, and he was being a little quiet and introspective. Rob seemed to notice this, and he leaned over and put his arm around David's shoulder.

"You didn't want to be intern, did you?" Rob said.

"Um . . . ," David said.

"Okay, I am intern, but you can be . . . assistant. Yay! David the assistant. Not as good, but still good, right?"

Rob exhaled a nice cloud of smoke into David's ear, and then turned around to watch the group of girls going crazy over their idol. As he watched and smoked, he seemed to be muttering something about a gold mine underneath his breath.

"They don't take reservations here," I said, after about half an hour of being jostled in the entryway of Freeman's. "Otherwise, we wouldn't have to wait like this."

Flan shrugged to let me know she didn't mind all that much. Freeman's is this quasi-secret restaurant at the end of an alley off the Bowery. Like all quasi-secret venues, it got hot immediately, and now it is overrun by celebrities and party kids and plenty of grown-ups trying to reclaim their youth. It's decorated in a sort of neo-hunting lodge style, with taxidermied animal heads and things like that on the walls. I'm basically against this kind of ostentatious cruelty to animals, but then I do own many, many pairs of leather shoes, so who am I to talk? As usual, the restaurant was full of people getting happy and loud and confessing all the horror stories of their busy days.

"Jonathan for two?!" the visibly stressed-out

hostess called, and when I nodded she waved me over to a table in the corner. It was dimly lit over there, in a kind of romantic, hidden way, and I couldn't help but say, as we took our seats, "See, even if we have to wait, they still always save me the best table."

Flan nodded and looked around, almost like she'd never seen so many people in one place before. Which of course she had. In New York even someone kind of innocent-seeming like Flan grows up quick.

I leaned back, thinking maybe things were finally looking up, when I realized they definitely were not.

The table across from us was filled with a particularly raucous party. It was Arno Wildenburger's crew. Arno himself was nowhere to be seen, but there were Rob and David, and Mimi Rathbone and her girlfriends, and some other people I didn't recognize, but who looked very, very hot. David was wearing the saffron Perry Ellis blazer I had contemplated buying that afternoon, and a faded black T-shirt that gave it a very downtown feel. That outfit was cooler than anything I'd ever seen him wear. He had his arm draped around that Sadie girl, and he looked hip and confident. He looked . . . Arno-ish.

"David looks a little out of his element, doesn't he?" I said dryly.

"He looks like he's having fun," Flan replied.

I decided I better go to the men's room and make sure I looked sufficiently cool. I kissed Flan on the cheek and told her I'd be right back. Then I stood waiting in front of the men's room, which was locked. After about five minutes, I pounded on the door and called out, "You want me to call an ambulance?"

The door cracked, and I saw Mimi Rathbone's friend Lizzie looking angry and a little flushed. "What the hell do you want?" she said.

Then Arno peaked his head over her. In spite of the fact that I'd just interrupted him and a girl, he seemed happy to see me. "Hey, J!" he said, pushing past Lizzie and doing the guy handclasp thing with me. "You hold that thought, gorgeous," he said over his shoulder. Then he closed the door behind him and stepped into the small waiting area. "What's up, man?"

I couldn't help but say, "Weren't you going out with that chick Mimi before?"

"Uh, kind of. This Hottest Private School Boy thing is crazy, man; it's like they can't get enough of me. It's all I can do to spread myself around."

126

"You mean you've been hooking up with Mimi *and* Lizzie all this time?"

"And Sadie. Although, now that you mention it, we haven't hooked up since yesterday afternoon sometime." He looked genuinely concerned. "I wonder if she feels left out. . . ."

I rolled my eyes at that.

"I'm planning a way to make it up to them all, though." Arno had apparently not noticed my disgust.

"Oh yeah?"

"Yeah," Arno said, lowering his voice. "Sometime early next week, when the issue is off the stands and everything has cooled down somewhat. My energy is just too in demand right now. But I think Monday night I'm going to invite all three of the girls to some hotel room. Those girls love each other. They love me. I'll definitely make it up to them."

"Make it up to them?" I said, dumbfounded.

"Yeah, you know, give 'em something to write about in their diaries."

"Oh," I said. Arno winked at me. There was a banging from the other side of the bathroom door, and then Arno saluted me and slipped back inside the bathroom to fool around with Lizzie.

I was so stunned by the level of ego craziness that he had achieved, that I forgot my original mission and stumbled back toward our table. When I saw that Flan was gone, I got that sick feeling all over again.

After all, if Arno was commanding that kind of action, David could certainly . . . well, I didn't even want to *think* about that. And there indeed was Flan, standing near Arno & Co.'s table, whispering something into David's ear.

I'd been pushed around enough that night. I marched over, and put my arm around Flan's waist.

"Excuse me," I said, "I think this is my date. And David? You should really work on getting your own look. Everyone knows you're just banking on Arno's reflected glory, so the least you could do is have a little self-respect and not dress like him."

Then I wheeled Flan around and hurried her back to our table.

another long night comes to an end for david

David stumbled into the kitchen of the West Village apartment he shared with his parents, hoping to find a snack. They had spent many hours at Lit, so it had been a while since he'd had that wild boar entrée at Freeman's. There had also been a lot of dancing since then. He was starving.

He flipped on the light in the kitchen, and dove into the refrigerator. He came back out with a container of deli macaroni and cheese and some salami slices.

That's when he saw his dad.

"Howdy," Sam Grobart said. He was sitting at the kitchen table in his bathrobe, reading *Psychoanalyst Weekly*, which was weird, because until David had come in the lights had been off.

"Hi, Dad."

"Where you been, son?"

"Um, Arno's house," David said, lying instinctively even though he knew his dad wouldn't care that he'd been out. To his dad, it was all just "experience."

"So . . . how's everything going?"

David sat down at the table with a sigh, and chewed thoughtfully on some salami. He knew better than to put off the emotional weather report. "Okay, I guess."

"Just okay?" Sam Grobart asked, putting down the paper.

"Things are weird with my friends, I guess. Or, with Jonathan, really. Ever since that party at the MoMA, he's been totally strange to me."

"How, exactly?"

"He's mean."

"Mmm, perhaps he's jealous."

"But of what? That whole Flan thing blew over ages ago," David said dramatically.

"You know, David, this is probably difficult for you to believe, but sometimes men can be more jealous over each other than over the women in their life. After all, you have all been friends for years. The girls just come and go. Try and think about what's making him act this way. . . ."

"Maybe he's jealous that I'm hanging out with Arno so much?"

"Perhaps."

"But that's not even that perfect. I mean, at first it was fun to be sort of celebrity-like, you know?" David slumped down in his seat a little. "And to feel cool for once. But then . . . this strange thing happened."

"What kind of strange thing?"

"Well, I don't know, Arno's a force of nature right now, I guess. And I worry that I'm, you know, just following him around."

"Mmmmm . . ."

"And the girls we've been hanging out with . . ."

"Yes, Mimi Rathbone and her friends. I was just talking to Mrs. Rathbone about this during our morning session. She is very relieved that the girls are in the tabloids for going out with boys their own age for once."

"Yeah, well, it's not all that wholesome. I mean, Arno's basically hooking up with all three of the girls all the time."

"Ah, so you're angry that he poached your mate?"

"Huh?" This was why David hated talking to his dad when he was quasi-drunk. It could get confusing and bizarre. Plus, his dad always made everything sound so animal kingdom-y. "Um, not really. I actually didn't care so much. But it's kind of nasty. And Fl—someone told me this secret tonight. Those girls were just having this competition to see who could hook up with Arno the most while his face was still on newsstands all around town."

"That *is* untoward."

David shrugged. "I'm just glad I found out. Now I

know not to hook up with Sadie. She wasn't really my type, anyway."

"Perhaps there's someone else?"

David took a few spoonfuls of the mac and cheese. "Well, I did meet this girl last Thursday . . ."

"Mmm-hmmm . . ."

"She's just different. Like, she looks like she walked out of a painting. She's just nothing like the girls we've been hanging out with. But I haven't seen her since then, and I guess I sort of gave up on ever seeing her again."

"This sounds like a very admirable goal, young man. Something different, something off the beaten path. Love transforms the soul, you know."

That was a bit much for David. "Uh, I think I just have to go to bed . . . ," he said.

He tossed the remainders of his snack into the trash can, turned off the light, and hurried to his bedroom, leaving his dad to read *Psychoanalyst Weekly* in the dark.

"Hi, um, this is David. Leave a message, and I'll get you back. Um, how do you? Mmph . . ." BEEP.

"Allo, Assistant *Daveed*. It is Intern Rob. Thursday morning, oh-nine-hundred hours. I have put on flyers at Gissing, Potterton, and Barton Day. Ooo, by le way do you have ten thousand dollars on you? I found the venue, a loft on Chelsea, and gigantic it is! But I need to pay deposit today, and it is ten thousand dollars. Call me, okay?"

"Hi, um, this is David. Leave a message, and I'll get you back. Um, how do you? Mmph . . ." BEEP.

"Allo, c'est moi. Oh-nine-hundred-thirty hours. Please to disregard last message."

i have never found parties this unattractive

To distract myself from the possibility that I was being cheated on (denial is always the best course, right?), I went to school again for all of Thursday. Well, almost all of it. See, by that afternoon there was a buzz. It wasn't exactly about me, but it wasn't exactly good for me, either.

I hadn't seen Arno all week, even though we both go to Gissing. I *had* been asked several times where he was, mostly by blushing girls who then asked if I could give him their numbers. I'd been brushing them off, all irritated-like—and that only seemed to make them want Arno more. But it really *was* starting to make me sick. And what was he going to do with those numbers, anyway? He certainly had his hands full with Mimi, Lizzie and Sadie.

And then, right before sixth period English lit, when I went to get my copy of *Othello* out of my locker, I got the news flash. There was Sandra

Anderson, standing next to me, looking very eager. Sandra goes to Barton Day, the girls' school next door, and she's really nice, if you know what I mean. She's plain and she has this plain group of friends who are all very nice, but you just know they sit around at home on weekends and bemoan the lack of boys in their lives and eat cake frosting.

Did that sound mean? Well, sorry. I was feeling pretty freaking mean.

Anyway, there I was, just trying to get to class and not think too much about anything, and suddenly there's Sandra, in my school, with this big, everything's-guh-reat smile on her face.

"Jonathan," she said, sort of swaying to the right like she had to pee, "you *must* tell me everything about the HPSB party. I *have* to get in. Can you get me in?"

"Um . . . what HPSB party?" I said very, very slowly.

"Oh, Jonathan, I know that you have to, like, limit access to your friend now because of all the demand for him these days, but you don't understand. Me and my friends are *such* Arno fans. Will you please, pretty please get me on the list?"

I must have gone a little pale or something, because Sandra's smile went away right then.

"I'll see what I can do . . . ," I said as steadily as I could manage, and then I said something about being late for class. "You should get back to Barton, too. If they catch you here, you'll be in trouble." Then I tried very hard to get down the hall without tripping or otherwise humiliating myself.

I clutched my *Othello* like a security blanket.

I meant to go to class, I really did. But once I'd turned the corner, I saw that the entire second floor west side hall was covered in flyers that said ARNO! and featured a picture of him shirtless. I was filled with the kind of manic desperation that demands you abandon all routine activity and do something, anything. I looked left, I looked right, and I ripped one of those freakish flyers down.

Underneath the (tacky) picture of Arno, it said COME CELEBRATE THE HOTTEST PRIVATE SCHOOL BOY OF 2005, AT THE HOTTEST PARTY OF 2005. The party was that Saturday at some loft in Chelsea. Apparently, the dress code was to be strictly enforced, and there was going to be a twenty-dollar door charge. And then underneath all that it said: AN EVENT PRODUCED BY ROB SANTANA, INTERN.

Now what did that mean? Did he have an internship I didn't know about? This was all just too weird. Weirder still, this seemed to be a major party. That I wasn't invited to.

There was no way in hell I was going to class now.

I ripped down a few more of the flyers, just to get out some of my anger at the whole insane world, and I blew right out of Gissing.

As I walked down 79th Street toward the subway, I called Flan. I think partly because I wanted to know that she wasn't with David, planning out what they would wear to the party that Saturday.

She picked up after three rings and sounded irritated. Apparently she was in history. I told her it was an emergency and that I needed to meet up with her, and she must have known things weren't right, because she said okay. She said she'd meet me at her house just as soon as she got out of class.

By the time Flan got to the Perry Street town house, I was sitting cross-legged on her bed upstairs, sort of meditation-like, and trying my best not to think the words "Hottest," "Private School," or "Arno."

When she walked through the door she kind of gasped in mock horror and said, "Baby, are you all right?"

"Yes. No. . . . Hey, you look good, Flannie," I said. And she did, too. Her hair was down and a little bit messy, and she was wearing these old faded Levi's that fit her perfectly, with a girly cardigan that was really stretched around the chest area. Flan's breasts were still growing all the time, and it seemed like she needed a whole new wardrobe almost weekly.

She smiled and came over and put her arms around me. "What's wrong?" she asked again, and I started telling her about how unbelievable and irritating it was that Arno had been named HPSB instead of me. We had had this conversation, of course, but I was finding it strangely satisfying to have it over and over again. Flan didn't really say anything, she just started making out with me. That felt really good, and for a while it took my mind off shit. Flan was being aggressive almost, in this way she'd never been before, which was nice. She kept running her fingers through my hair, and kind of pulling at the edges of my clothes.

But I couldn't totally stop thinking about the HPSB party, and eventually that led me to think of Rob, and that led to David.

And then I stupidly said: "How far did you go with David last winter?"

"*What?*" Flan jumped up and gave me this look. There it was: that look was the low point of a really, really low day. She started re-buttoning her cardigan. "Jonathan, what is wrong with you lately?"

I sat up and put my face in my hands. "I'm sorry, Flan," I said. "I'm really not *me* lately. This whole thing with Arno being named Hottest Private School Boy . . . and how my clique is sort of falling out . . . and, there's a party. It's so irritating and pathetic, but Arno's throwing a party to celebrate his own HPSB-ness, and . . ."

"This Saturday? Yeah, I know," Flan said.

"How do you know?"

"Cuz Rob invited me," she said with a shrug. Then she walked out of the room, and downstairs. She called back something about whether I was staying for dinner or not.

But all I could think about was the fact that Rob had invited Flan. Had he invited her at David's request? Was this all part of David's big scheme to get Flan back? Did he have some big thing planned to win her back at the "hottest" party of the year?

It was so heart-crushingly obvious. He totally did.

"Wildenburger, talk to me." BEEP.

"Arno, it is Rob, Thursday afternoon. I have papered the walls of your school with flyers announcing the party in your honor. There is such . . . how you say . . . buzz. I cannot wait for the big night. Oh, and one other thing. Do you know this girl, Sandra Anderson? She is maybe a head shorter than I, but she says she has many friends. Is it true? Let me know. Ciao baby."

"Hello, it is Rob. Bueno, es Rob. Allo, c'est Rob. Digame." BEEP.

"Hey, Rob, it's Arno. That's all great news, great news. Listen, I've got another intern task for you to do. I'm arranging for a very special evening for me and all the girls. Hope this isn't a blow to you—I know you were kind of with Lizzie for a minute. But see, there's only one Hottest Private School Boy, if you know what I mean, so no hard feelings, right? Anyway, what I want you to do is, have invitations printed up at Tiffany's, one for each of the girls. Get a pen, and write this down: *You are invited to the Hottest Private Party of 2005, at the W Hotel, this Monday at midnight. Ask for the Wildenburgers' usual suite at the front desk.* Okay? And have them hand delivered Saturday afternoon with a dozen roses. Got that? Thanks."

"Hello, it is Rob. Bueno, es Rob. Allo, c'est Rob. Digame."
BEEP.
"Hi, um, is this Rob Santana? Yeah, hi, this is Lily Maynard from Barton Day's chapter of Homeless Outreach? I got your number off the Hottest Private School Boy party flyer, and I was wondering if you had anything to do with putting them up. Because whoever did tore down all the flyers for our big fund-raising event this Saturday. It took us all morning to put them up, and printing all those flyers cost a quarter of our budget for this semester. So I guess what I'm trying to say is that whoever did this is going to pay—not for our flyers, although you'll pay for that, too, but *really* pay, you know what I'm saying?"

Even by Mickey Pardo standards, it was early to be at
Max Fish. Or, the Fish, as he had been calling his
favorite Ludlow Street bar since second semester freshman year.

But Mickey was currently a man with a mission, and
it was a mission that had so far met with extremely
limited success. All day at school, he had hyped his
naked restaurant vision to classmates; it had earned him
nothing more than vacant stares, quasi-promises to
attend by a few burnout dudes, and one trip to the
principal's office.

Even his guys weren't really with him on it. Arno,
David, and Patch hadn't even returned his calls, and
Jonathan had said he'd love to do it, unconvincingly,
but he felt kind of weird bringing Flan to an event with
nudity—she was still in eighth grade, after all. That was
his excuse.

Mickey was belly-up to the bar by five o'clock,

nursing a Tecate and tequila happy hour special and trying to figure out what he was doing wrong.

There was no one in the bar but the bartender, three girls in Interpol T-shirts who were talking about how to meet more guys in bands, and him. It was pretty well lit, and all the bright circuslike decorations looked a little sad in the almost daylight. Mickey looked at the dude behind the bar and said, "You would get naked in a restaurant, wouldn't you? I mean, for the sake of art. You'd do that, right?"

The bartender pulled at the sleeves of his faded black T-shirt, and tried to brush the greasy bangs out of his eyes. He appeared to be thinking. "Yeah, man," he said at last. Then he added, a little sadly, "I used to go to art school."

"So you'll be there? It's a week from today, at twilight, at that joint Fresh on Gansevoort." That was the closest to a yes Mickey had gotten all day, and it made him feel like another tequila shot.

"Yeah," the bartender said flatly, "I'll be there."

"Well, that's kind of a relief. That means there'll be two of us."

The bartender looked nervous all of a sudden. "You mean, just you and me?"

"Hey, man, don't trip, I'm not gay or anything. It just ain't easy getting people on board with this thing."

Both Mickey and the bartender thought about that for a long minute. The bartender poured them each a shot, and after they'd downed them, he said, "I have an idea."

"What is it?"

"You know how in skin flicks, lesbian chicks are always dying to get naked?"

"Really?" Mickey said. "I guess I never noticed that."

"Yeah, like in orgy scenes or whatever, they're always, like, natural—what do you call them?—exhibitionists."

"Oh."

"So that's perfect," the bartender enthused. "Go get some lesbians, dude!"

They did another shot, and Mickey thought about it. Lesbians *did* seem more open about sexuality and bodies and stuff, although he wasn't sure pornos were the best evidence of that, but still, by the time the tequila had burned a hot streak down his insides, he was completely psyched on the idea.

He stood up and slapped the bar. "I'm going to get some lesbians, man!"

"Awesome. I'm Jason, by the way." He stuck out his hand at Mickey.

"Mickey. I'll see you next Thursday?"

"Sure, brah," Jason said. He even seemed to mean it.

It was getting dark. Mickey was definitely feeling way

up now. He walked across Houston to Meow Mix, which he remembered February mentioning all the time during her brief lesbian period a few years ago.

When he got there, he saw that it looked more or less like any other bar: dark, a little dirty, with a full wall of liquor bottles all aglow. The only difference was that the girls way outnumbered the dudes.

Mickey was relieved to see this girl Petra, whom he went to school with, sitting on a couch close to the door. She had dreads wound into a big, neat bun on the top of her head. He went over and sat down next to her.

"Hey, Petra," he said.

"Mickey!" she said. She looked nervous to see him, which struck Mickey as odd since she'd come out as bi their freshman year. "What's up?"

"Nothing much. Hey, how would you like to pose naked in a restaurant? Everyone else would be naked, too."

Petra's eyes narrowed. "Is that your way of hitting on me, Mickey Pardo? Because you know I know your girlfriend. Or ex-girlfriend. Or whatever's going on with you two."

"Is that a no?" Mickey said.

Petra nodded.

Unfazed, Mickey said, "Damn, well, catch ya later," and went to find someone else to pitch his concept to.

He picked a girl with a lot of metal in her face, who was standing near the door. He approached her and said, "Hey, would you like to get naked in a restaurant?"

The girl gave him a long, cool stare. "Get lost," she said.

Well, that wasn't going to work. Mickey wasn't really the kind of guy to give up, though, so he went to the end of the bar and warmed up for a different kind of sales pitch.

He ordered a Negro Modelo and a vodka cran from the bartender. She set them in front of him, and disappeared with his money.

Mickey turned to the girl on the stool next to him and tapped her shoulder. He had to do it twice, because she was making out with the girl sitting next to her. When she turned, he pushed the vodka cran in her direction. "Hey, I bought this for you."

The girl gave him a look that might have been disgust. She looked weirdly familiar. Her hair was an almost white shade of blond, and it was cut in little bangs across her forehead, and her skin had a kind of orange tone to it. She was wearing a very short skirt. Mickey decided that he probably didn't recognize her, it was just that she looked really, really out of place in a bar like this. She took the drink and sniffed it.

"What, did you ruf me?" she said.

"No way, I need you alive and kickin'." Mickey cackled to himself, not knowing how what he'd just said sounded out loud. He proceeded anyway: "But I would like you to come to my naked restaurant event. It's a Luc Vogel-inspired tableau of a naked crowd, dining at Fresh, and . . ."

"Oh, that place on Gansevoort where they only serve cold food?" The blonde's face became notably brighter. "I *adore* Fresh."

"What the fuck?" The girl on the other side of the blonde stood up, knocking her stool back to the ground. She twisted around to get a look at Mickey. "You picking up on my date, ass—" but she didn't finish what she was saying, because that's when she saw that Mickey was Mickey, and Mickey saw that she was . . .

Philippa.

The blonde in the middle had a very big uh-oh look on her face. She got off her bar stool and said, "You guys probably have to talk. But it was nice to finally meet you, Mickey. My name's Sadie, and *definitely* let me know about the Fresh event."

Mickey didn't wait until she was out of earshot to say, "Were you just making out with that girl?"

Philippa rolled her eyes and nodded.

"Because that's kind of hot. And if you want to experiment, that's cool. But maybe you shouldn't do it

147

in public. And it would have been nice if we'd talked about it beforehand, you know what I mean?"

Philippa put her hands on both of Mickey's shoulders.

"Don't you get it?" she said, shaking her head sadly. "I really *am* gay."

Several hours later, Mickey was at the Fish again. There were lots of people now, and they all looked very thin and bored. And blurry. Mickey wasn't sure how he'd ended up here, but there was one thing he couldn't get out of his head.

His girlfriend wasn't into having boyfriends anymore.

patch and flan have a heart-to-heart

After Jonathan left, Flan came up to Patch's giant room and lay down in the hammock. Neil Young was playing quietly in the background, and Patch was wearing those same khakis and one of the hundreds of skateboarding T-shirts that he'd been given for free when all the skateboarding companies were courting him to go pro. She didn't say anything, so after a while, Patch said, "What's wrong, little sis?"

He put down the *Lonely Planet Afghanistan* that he had been flipping through all evening, and watched her fidget for a minute. The Christmas lights that he'd strung up around his room cast a warm light on her face as she thought about how best to respond.

"It's just that . . . I always wanted to be Jonathan's girlfriend *so bad*, you know?" she sighed. "And now that I finally am, things just aren't going so well."

"Every relationship has its rough spots," Patch said. The phrase sounded hollow in his voice. He didn't really know what he was talking about—Patch had never stayed in a relationship long enough to experience the rough spots. But he felt like he'd heard people say this before, probably David, and it seemed like better advice than telling his little sister to dump one of his best friends.

"I know," said Flan. "But it's just like it's always about *him* and *his* social life. Sometimes I feel like I'm just along for the ride. Does that make sense? I just wonder if maybe I'm giving up too much."

"Hey, Flannie, Jonathan adores you, you know that, right?" Patch said. "But it seems like he's not at the top of his game lately. Just be sure that's not why you're considering breaking up with him, okay?"

"Okay," Flan said, "I promise."

"There's something else on your mind, too, huh?" Patch asked, pushing the hammock so it started swinging gently.

"Um, well . . . it's just that Jonathan's stepbrother, Rob, keeps calling me. He says that David wants to hook up with me."

"Rob's been calling *you*?" Patch said. "I mean . . . do you get the feeling David has a crush on you?"

Flan shrugged. "Not really."

"Yeah, I don't think he does, either. At least, I don't think after what happened last winter he'd ever act on it for Jonathan's sake, even if you and J did break up. And you don't like David, do you?"

"Of *course* I don't like David."

"See, that shit pisses me off," Patch said with more feeling than he'd had in a while.

"Oh, calm down, Dad." Flan always thought it was amusing when her older brother got all protective. "And I hung out with Rob and Feb while you were in Europe, so him calling isn't that out of the blue. It's more that . . . if things are weird with J and me, I don't want any rumors going around."

Patch got off the couch and came the closest to pacing he'd ever been in his life. "That guy's got to be stopped," he said. "He's pure evil."

"Well, I think he's just, you know, European," Flan mused. "Like, creepy, kind of."

"Nah, it's more than that. I think he's a bad influence. I mean, look how crazy all my guys are acting! I'm just worried about them. I think Rob's made everybody worry about being cool way too much."

Flan smiled in her secret Flan way. "But you guys have *always* been cool."

Patch shook his head. "Maybe, but it's never been this stressful. I think Rob's riding the *New York* magazine thing for his own purposes somehow. Like him calling you about David? He's not trying to set you up. What's the point in that? I think he's fucking with Jonathan."

Flan thought about that a moment. Then she noticed something odd. "Hey, big brother?"

"Yup?"

"Why are you reading a travel book about Afghanistan?"

"I dunno." Patch sank back into the couch and tried to think of a way to explain his troubles. "I need something to need," he said slowly.

"Is that like some anti-zen motto?" Flan giggled.

"Can you keep a secret?"

Flan clutched the edge of the hammock and nodded seriously.

"I've been depressed all week, ever since the night of the MoMA party. I got all these calls from that Justine person that day—"

"You mean, Justine Gray of *New York*?" Flan asked darkly.

"Yes, that one. She left me all these messages about how cool I was, and how the magazine wanted to do a profile on me, and she said that—"

"Wait, hold up, mister. You mean *New York* wanted *you* to be Hottest Private School Boy?"

"I guess, but that's not really the point."

"I know, but that's just crazy. Especially because of all the drama. . . ." Flan drifted off and appeared to be processing the enormity of it all. "Weird," she said.

"I know. But the worst thing was, on the message she left she had this whole complex justification for why I was hottest whatever. She said that it was because I didn't want anything or need anything." Patch paused as though even the memory of it caused him pain. "She called me an island."

"Oh," Flan said. She looked very sad. She obviously got it.

"And so I've been trying all these things, looking for something to really want and care about, and I just can't find anything that holds my attention. It's driving me crazy. I think the only thing I can really do is become a war correspondent. You know, shock myself with experience from the big, bad world."

Flan rolled off the hammock, and came over to Patch and hugged him. "That's all pretty heavy, big bro." She shook her head and added, "But no way am I letting you go to Afghanistan."

"I might have to, though."

"But there must be *something*," she said brightly.

"I've really wracked my brain, kiddo."

"When was the last time you were happy—like, really, really happy?"

Patch shook his head. "I can't even remember."

Flan kissed him on the cheek. "Well, I'm going to bed. This is too much depression and gloom for me in one night. But I'm going to think of something, don't you worry."

When Flan was gone, Patch tried to think about what happy meant. Maybe he had never really been happy, and his whole life had been a fruitless quest for some little bit of satisfaction.

He closed his eyes and thought *happy* over and over again, and what came into his head was the morning he woke up with Greta on the *Ariadne*. She had been so alive and awesome: She told off the RA who had been hitting on Patch, and then somehow there had been roses in the bed and they had fooled around and talked for the rest of the day, and Patch had felt completely understood and relaxed and . . . happy.

And then she'd come back to New York with him and she'd been so entirely cool—she was just down for whatever. She was probably the only person on the planet who didn't mind walking forty blocks or so, and she thought Coney Island was as cool as he did, and she never whined about the water being dirty, or the beach being too crowded, and she actually liked fried clams, which was something he'd *never* known a girl to like.

Of course, eventually she'd had to go back to California for school, and Patch had thought at first that was probably a good thing, because he'd always thought of himself as kind of a loner. But maybe nothing had been right since she'd left. Maybe he wasn't so much of a loner after all. Now, when he thought about it, "loner" was just another way of calling somebody an island. And calling somebody an island just wasn't nice.

Patch thought about Greta all night. By the time the sun was coming up on Perry Street, he had located his ID and called a car to take him to the airport. He'd finally thought of something that he really wanted.

David had been laying low, going to basketball practice and doing his homework. Then, Friday afternoon, when he was leaving school, he got a call from Rob saying that he should head over to the hotel bar at 66 Thompson for an after-work drink.

David wasn't sure what Rob meant by "work," and he didn't really want to go anywhere near Rob right then. But he had been replaying the five minutes of his life that he'd spent in the glow of the Modigliani over and over, and she had become an obsession. He had even started playing tricks on himself that involved her. For instance, when he was practicing free throws, he told himself that if he made fifteen shots in a row, that meant he would run into her again that weekend. He told himself that if he finished his trig homework in less than half an hour, she was thinking about him, too. If he could get all the way from his house to school without once thinking of her, they were meant to be.

But he'd finally realized (somewhere between home

and school) that he wasn't going to get to see her again by playing stupid mind games. He was actually going to have to go out. And that was how he ended up at 66 Thompson on Friday evening, watching Rob talk into his cell phone.

They were seated in low little armchairs at a small glass table with a candle on it. The room was all warm and muted, and it had several of these small tables surrounded by low chairs. A jazz trio was softly plucking away in the corner. David guessed this was what they called a lounge.

He took a sip of Stella and looked around. There were a lot of business guys loosening their ties and European tourists talking animatedly. The Modigliani was not there.

When Rob got off the phone he made a noise like he was exhausted.

"What are we doing here?" David asked.

"Well, to people-watch the beautiful people!" Rob said, taking a gulp of his Campari and Sprite. He was wearing a black cardigan, white dress shirt, and flooding khakis. David was amazed that any guy under seventy-five would actually try to pull off a cardigan.

Rob seemed very into everything, though: He was snapping his fingers to the music. "Plus, the party on the roof here at 66 Thompson, it is one of the hottest in the city. I want to get some, how you say . . . tips when it starts later on."

"Tips?" David said.

"Yes, for the fabulouso party tomorrow night."

"Oh."

There was a long, awkward silence, during which David focused on his beer. Rob broke it by jumping out of his chair and yelling, "Sandra!"

He ran over to a girl who had just come through the door and was looking around awkwardly. He gave her a kiss on each cheek, and led her back over to their table.

"David, this is Sandra Anderson, Sandra, this is David," Rob said.

David recognized Sandra from parties and around. She was a little bit moonfaced and chesty, in a pretty way, and she was wearing an outfit straight out of the J.Crew catalog. Even David could recognize that.

They talked about school and the friends they had in common and which parties they'd seen each other at lately. When the waiter came, she ordered a vodka and tonic.

Rob seemed to have forgotten all about Mimi, Lizzie, and Sadie. He had his hands all over Sandra, and he was making her blush and giggle. Then her cell rang, and she excused herself to talk to her friend. Before she left she whispered something into Rob's ear that made him smile.

David thought it was sort of cool that Rob would hang out with a girl so un-It, and he tried to think of a way to say that. But before he got a chance, Rob leaned toward him and said, conspiratorially, "You know, she has lots of friends."

"Um, really? I guess I don't know who she hangs out with."

"Yes, beaucoup friends."

Rob smiled in a self-satisfied way. David didn't know if it was his clouded headspace right then, or that it was the end of a long week or what, but Rob was really starting to get on his nerves. "So what," he said.

"You don't think I'm really interested in *Sandra,* do you?" Rob giggled as he continued. "She is super uncool and a little ugly, no? See, she has so many friends and they all come to party tomorrow night! They are all going to come and pay the door charge."

"Huh?"

"Oh, David, this is the life of intern. You have no idea how many super uncool and a little bit ugly girls I have smooched in the last week just to get them to come to this party. But what an event it will be!"

David thought he might be sick.

He excused himself and hurried to the bathroom. Before he could get there, though, he saw Jonathan talking to the hostess. Flan was standing next to him.

David was filled with relief—Jonathan would know how to handle sick and twisted Rob. And his dad had, after all, advised him to find a way to make up. David raised his hand to wave in their direction, but when he saw the look on Jonathan's face he panicked. From the way he was grimacing, it looked like Jonathan didn't want to see David at all.

David turned and hurried in the other direction.

**i try and reclaim the old days,
when i was still hot**

If I needed any more evidence that David was really and truly after my girl—and not just "insanely attracted" to her—then I got it Friday night, when he ran out of the lounge at 66 Thompson at the very sight of me and Flan together.

I shook my head, and then told the hostess, "Yeah, a place by the balcony would be best."

Rob waved at us, and I waved back. He raised his hands as if to say, "Well isn't this a coincidence." I nodded at him, but I was pretty sure that it was no coincidence at all. I mean, it was just a few hours earlier when he had come into my room and asked me where I was getting all dressed up to go. That's when I told him that I loved this bar, and how hot the roof party that they throw at night is, and how I was taking Flan there for a bite to eat that night.

We sat down, and Flan put her jacket over the back of her chair.

"Can you believe Rob is here?" I said. "I mean, it was practically five minutes ago that I told him this place was hot."

"Yeah, crazy," Flan said, examining her cuticles.

"Hold on," I told her. I quickly called Mickey and Patch to see if they wanted to come hang out with us, but neither of them picked up. I left them messages, and told them it looked like a fun night. Then I turned all my attention to Flan.

"Thanks for coming out with me," I said. "I know I've been really obnoxious about the whole HPSB thing, and about that party tomorrow night. The whole thing is just disgusting to me. But this is exactly what I needed: Dress up, go out, not think too much about tomorrow and what it means."

Flan smiled enigmatically at me. "Thanks for being my boyfriend," she said. "Let's have fun tonight, okay?"

"Don't we always have fun?" I said as the waiter approached and waited to take our order. I couldn't resist adding: "But yeah, I made some calls, and there are some parties tonight that we should make an appearance at."

Then Flan ordered a ginger ale and a plate of French fries, and I ordered a Guinness. The waiter nodded and disappeared.

And I really thought for a moment, *This is nice. This feels human.* And when Rob came over, he still seemed friendly. I was grateful for that. I felt like maybe he was on my side.

"You two look gorgeous," he said.

"Thanks," Flan said.

"I mean, you really just make such a gorgeous couple," Rob repeated.

"Thanks, Rob," I said, trying to slip Flan an apologetic he's-a-freak look.

"So, you too are coming to my—I mean, Arno's party tomorrow, right?"

"Oh yeah, of course we're—" Flan started to say, but I interrupted her and finished her sentence: "—probably going to be busy." I almost felt bad. Rob was being so nice. But there was no way I was going to endure the humiliation of a party in the honor of that *other* Hottest Private School Boy. And especially not now that I knew David was going to try and steal my girl there. "Not that we wouldn't love to go," I added.

"Well, I put you both on the list, anyway," Rob said, making a sad-clown face. "You still both tell all your friends, right?"

"Yeah, sure," I said.

"Yours, too?" he said to Flan.

"Yeah, all my friends are really excited about going," Flan said. She seemed to say it more to me than to Rob.

"Bravo!" Rob said. Then he bit his lip like he'd thought of something bad. "Flan, you haven't had calls from David, have you?"

Flan's face got all cloudy then, and she said no, and excused herself to the bathroom really abruptly. Rob sat in her chair. "Brother," he said, "remember our conversation the other night? About David?"

"Uh-huh . . ."

"Well, I don't know anything for sure, but . . ." Rob waved over my shoulder at someone. I turned and saw a girl I thought was Sandra Anderson sitting at the table Rob had been sitting at. "I must go. But be careful, Jonathan."

And just like that, I knew that I wasn't going to be having any fun tonight.

Patch gave the woman at the Dollar Rent-A-Car his most winning smile, but she kept on shaking her head.

"I need a car, though, that's the thing," he said.

"Honey-bunch, you are *very* cute. But I just can't rent a car to anyone under eighteen years of age."

"I'll be eighteen in December."

"Mmm-hmm, six months? I don't think I can work with that."

Patch ran some fingers through his sandy hair and considered several options. He could say that his dad was right this moment flying in from New York and would be mostly driving the car, and that he, Patch, just wanted to impress Dad by picking him up in the car. He could pretend to call his mom on his cell phone, and pretend that she was in the hospital, or somewhere nearby, and pretend-promise to get there before she went under for an operation that has a thirty percent success rate. He could grab any random set of keys from behind the desk, and run out of there as fast as possible.

But for Patch, truthfulness and charm had always been the winning combination.

"Listen, the thing is, there's a girl . . ."

"Oh yeah?" The Dollar Rent-A-Car lady still had that cynical look on her face, but she was listening.

"She lives out here, and I live in New York. We met last winter, on a boat, and we were really into each other. We had the best time of our lives. But then we both had to go back where we belong, and . . ." Patch sighed. "Never mind."

"No, wait . . . what happens?"

"Nothing. I guess the story ends there."

"No, it can't. I mean . . . where is she?" Another woman had come up behind her and was now listening in.

"I don't know, that's the thing. She lives in Santa Cruz, that's all I know."

"Well, you have to go find her," the other woman said.

"But what if I can't find her?"

"You *have* to," the first woman said.

"How can I without a car?"

"Well, you can rent a car!"

"But where?"

"Right here, of course," the second woman said brightly.

"I'd really appreciate that."

"How about a free upgrade? You like Range Rovers?"

Half an hour later, Patch was stuck in traffic on 101 South. It was still early-ish on Friday afternoon, but somehow there were more cars than freeway out here. And there seemed to be a lot of freeway—miles and miles of it.

Forty-five minutes later, he was lost in the redwoods. At least he had gotten away from the cars, but he still didn't know where he was.

An hour after that, he had somehow located the city of Santa Cruz, and stood looking at its boardwalk. He found a telephone book and looked up the O'Gradys. There were five of them in the book, but he had either forgotten or never known Greta's parents' names and so had no idea which one was the O'Grady he was looking for. He ripped out the page, and got back into his rental Range Rover.

It took him another hour to find four out of the five houses, ask for Greta, and be told that he had the wrong house. The sun was going down by the time Patch pulled onto a quiet street of craftsman houses pretty near the beach, and knocked on the last O'Grady door on the white phone book page.

No one answered, and after a solid ten minutes of knocking, Patch was ready to quit. Maybe Greta was just someone he'd made up in his head after all.

But that was when he heard a very familiar trilling kind of laugh, somewhere nearby. He spun around, but there was nobody to be seen, so he stepped lightly off the stone path that led from the street to the door, and walked along the side of the house.

He could smell barbecuing and hear laughter and splashing. When he got to the end of the house, he peeked around to see a backyard with a swimming pool and a bunch of kids running around it and doing cannonballs off the diving board. He stepped out onto the patio, and that's when he saw Greta.

She was sitting on a lounge chair, wearing vans, jean cutoffs, and a bikini top, and she was even prettier and more relaxed-looking than he'd remembered. There was a guy sitting on the chair next to her, and he was whispering something into her ear that was cracking her up. Patch realized all of a sudden that he had no reason to think that Greta had been waiting around for him all this time. He took a step backward, but it was too late. She'd already seen him.

"Hey, Patch," she said with a calm, if slightly bemused, smile.

"Hey, Greta."

"What are you doing here?"

"I just wanted to see you, I guess."

"Well don't just stand there," she said. "Come over here and meet my big brother."

"Wildenburger, talk to me." BEEP.

"Rob the intern here. Just wanted you to know that I took care of the—ahem—special night. There will be flowers and invitations sent to the apartments of the lovely ladies this afternoon. And do not worry, monsieur, I get girls just from being your intern! Plenty girls to go around! Ciao."

"Hello, you have reached Rob Santana Productions. Please leave a message." BEEP.

"Hiya, uh, Rob Santana? This is Larry from City Parties. I got you down for ten kegs, five mixed boxes of spirits, five cases of wine, ten cases of champagne. It's Saturday morning, I'm at the address you gave me, and, uh, there's nobody here. . . . Give me a call and let me know what's going on."

"Hello, you have reached Rob Santana Productions. Please leave a message." BEEP.

"Hey, Rob. It's Sandra Anderson, remember me? Anyway, you disappeared from the roof party at 66 Thompson last night, and I haven't heard from you since, which was weird. I'm still coming to the party tonight, with all my friends like you asked. But I just want to know: Am I going to be humiliated and feel like an idiot around you all night? Are you a user, Rob?"

"Hi, this is Jonathan. Don't forget to leave your number if I don't have it." BEEP.
"Hey, J, it's Flan. So, after a night like last night, I'm afraid you're just going to have to take me to the Hottest Private School Boy party tonight. You know why? You dragged me around to all those miserable parties last night, and you stuck me with Liza Komansky for, like, half an hour of grilling about our relationship while you talked to some guy you aren't even friends with—thanks for that, by the way—and you were in a total mood all night. So tonight, we're doing something with *my* friends, okay? Be at my house at quarter of eight, and we can all go together. Love ya."

"Hello, you have reached Rob Santana Productions. Please leave a message." BEEP.
"Rob, it's Jonathan. Haven't seen you around the apartment lately. Guess I haven't been there much,

171

either. Just wanted to make sure I'm still on the list for the party tonight. I am, right?"

"Hi, this is Jonathan. Don't forget to leave your number if I don't have it." BEEP.

"J.M., it's your mother, Saturday morning. Where are you, darling? Did you let anyone in the apartment this morning? I just noticed that my Rolodex is missing from the home office, and so I did a very thorough search of the apartment, and nothing else seems to be missing except my ATM card. Jonathan, I can't think why you would take these things. You have money, don't you? I'm calling the bank now, but call me as soon as you get this, and let me know if you know anything. I'm absolutely out of my head."

I'm still not sure how I ended up agreeing to go to the Hottest Private School Boy party, against all my better judgment and also against my taste, although I know it had something to do with me being a bad boyfriend. As we all know, bad boyfriends can be compelled to do pretty much any crazy thing.

Flan told me to be at her house at quarter of eight, but I got there at half past nine, and all the girls in her inner circle were there already. Flan and I have talked a lot about how her clique is really similar to mine. They all go to different schools now, except Daria, whose mother is this quasi-famous real estate queen. Daria goes to Florence with Flan, and she's kind of haughty and entitled the way Arno is. And then there's Rachel—her parents work in publishing and she's very Upper West Side and seems to be at swim team practice all the time; and Gemma the wild party girl, whose mother is a famous socialite and whose dad is a haunted classical conductor type; and Kendall, who is really into fashion and small animals and being a vegetarian. She holds everybody together, and nobody really knows where her parents got their money.

I've never thought of Flan as being anything like Patch, but I saw a little bit of it when I came in that night. For starters, all her friends were already in her bedroom, doing girl stuff getting ready to go out, but she was nowhere in sight.

Kendall came up to me, gave me the three-cheek kiss treatment, and asked where Flan was. Her hair was all frizzy from the rain (it was pouring outside), but it worked because she was wearing Michael Kors sunglasses, even indoors. I told her I didn't know, and then she started telling me about how she'd just gotten an internship with Imitation of Christ for that summer, which I had to admit sounded pretty cool. I gave the twelve-pack of PBR that I'd bought for them to Gemma, who happily started distributing them around the room. Then she told me that I rocked. I wasn't exactly sure whether it was a good thing to buy beer for a bunch of eighth-graders, but in the end it seemed like what Flan would have wanted me to do.

Daria asked me about Mickey's event at Fresh, which she said she had heard about from her older sister who goes to school with Mickey. She seemed kind of psyched on it, but I told her I didn't think it was really going to happen. The idea of taking Flan to a restaurant and being naked with a lot of strangers, and a lot of people we knew really well, kind of freaked me out.

When Flan came in, she seemed almost shy of all these people in her house, even though they were her best friends. But they all kissed her and asked her where she'd been, and when she showed them the vintage Balenciaga sack dress she'd just found at Tokyo Joe's on East 10th, they all made *ooo* and *ahh* noises. It even seemed sweet to *me.*

"Isn't she just beautiful?" Gemma said, mostly to me, I think.

Flan pulled me aside, and we made out for a minute in the hall.

"You look nice," she said.

"Thanks." I'd gone for casual in a pinstriped A.P.C. blazer and these spectator loafers I've been into lately, but I was still glad that she'd noticed.

"I'm glad you agreed to go to the party," she said.

"Me, too," I said, although I was more just glad to see her. Going to the party, that part I was still dreading heavily.

It took us a while longer to get ready, and then we walked over to Seventh Avenue, hailed two cabs, and asked to be taken to The Awful Event. Especially if tonight was the night that David was planning on stealing Flan.

It was pretty obvious when we'd found the party. There was a line leading out the door, and upstairs, through big industrial windows, we could see what looked like a light show. Also, you could hear The Bravery playing at top volume, from what must have been pretty professional speakers, all the way from Eighth Avenue.

"Oh, I've been here before," Daria said as we stood on the curb considering how we were going to get past that crowd at the door. Nearly everyone waiting to get in the door was shielded by an umbrella, but they all looked pretty soaked, anyway.

"You have not, you East Side snob," Gemma said good-naturedly. She jumped up and down and clapped her hands when she said this.

"No, really. It belongs to a friend of my mom's.

He used to be in real estate, too. He bought this place when Chelsea was still cheap and built it out from scratch to be his apartment. But then he realized he could make way more just renting it out for parties. Mom says it's *obscene* what he gets for it."

I wondered, not for the first time, how Rob had pulled this off.

We walked closer, and the girls stood at what seemed to be the end of the line.

I try never to wait on lines, so I told the girls to sit tight, and that I would see what I could do. All the soaked kids with their dangerously jutting umbrellas shot me foul looks as I pushed my way up to the door. When I got there I saw that the line went all the way up the stairs to the second story.

"Hey, man," said a guy who I'm pretty sure wasn't in high school anymore. He was wearing a dirty jean jacket over dirty jeans, and he had longish stringy hair. I think he might have been one of the Backseat Rockstars, like the bassist maybe. He blocked my way and said, "There's no way you're cutting into this line."

This pissed me off, but what was I going to do, fight with a Backseat Rockstar? I went back to where Flan and her friends were, shivering under umbrellas, and told them that the place was at capacity and—for legal reasons that had nothing to do with our relative hotness—they were letting people in slowly.

Forty-five minutes later, when we got to the top of those stairs, we were all a little bit cranky and a little bit soaked. There was a big guy taking money at the door, and maybe I let a little too much of my crankiness show.

"Hi," I said curtly. "Jonathan M. plus two, Flan F. plus two."

"Both plus two, huh? Everyone thinks they're on the list tonight," the door guy said, chuckling to himself. He took a long time looking up and down his clipboard. "Yeah," he said, "I'm really not seeing your names here."

"Well, look again," I said. Then I added, idiotically, "I'm Rob Santana's brother."

"Now there's one thing I hate, and it's a liar," the door guy said.

"*Excuse me?*" I said, "What's your name again?"

"It's Chino," he said. "And that's the truth. Wanna know something else? You sure *ain't* Rob Santana's brother."

I could hear Gemma behind me, giggling. "Jonathan, just pay him, okay?"

"That's going to be twenty dollars for you and all your little friends," Chino said.

"That's outrageous!" I said.

"Jonathan, can we just go in?" Flan said.

Daria stepped up to Chino and opened her wallet. She pulled out seven twenties and handed them over. "Don't ever call my girls 'little friends' again, got that?" she said, pointing a French-manicured fingernail at Chino. "Oh, and one of those is for you, tough guy."

Then somehow we got ushered into this big room that was full of noise and music and people who weren't wearing a whole lot of clothing. It was happening in there, but pretty much all I could think about was how embarrassing getting into the party was.

"What was up that guy's ass?" I said loudly enough that Flan's crew of girlfriends heard me above the blaring music. "Can you believe we weren't on the list? I mean, who wants to go to this lame party, anyway?"

They all stopped and stared at me, and then turned to Flan with faces full of . . . pity, I think it was.

"I mean, don't they know who I am?" I added, pathetically.

"Hey, Jonathan," Kendall said. "Maybe you should relax and try to have a little fun, okay?"

When Arno had woken up at around one on Saturday, he had more messages than he really thought he could listen to, and Mimi had already left. His room still smelled like her, though—she was working on developing her own fragrance, tentatively called Mi, and so she had been trying out a different sample every day. This one smelled kind of like jasmine and sex.

He stood in front of the mirror, twisting his retro Confederate cap to just the right angle, and then he heard a car honking downstairs. It was probably time to head over to West 20th Street and see what Rob had come up with. He leaned out the window and saw that Mimi was waiting for him in her parents' town car. He walked out of the house without grabbing anything. What did he need? He was Arno fucking Wildenburger.

"Hey, Mims," he said when he got to the car.

"It's Lizzie," said Lizzie. She was wearing perhaps the coyest smile that Arno had ever seen, and a black suede skirt that was even shorter than Mimi's black suede skirt.

Her hair was pulled back tight into a high *I Dream of Jeannie*-style ponytail. "Get in," Lizzie said.

Arno got in. Lizzie poured them each a rocks glass of Alize. "Here's to your party," she said. Arno hadn't realized until right then that Lizzie had the same soft, fuzzy voice that Mimi had. He raised his glass, and they made a little clinking noise.

"Did you get the invitation?" Arno said.

"Uh-huh. You're pretty hot, Arno Wildenburger. We're considering it. But in the meantime, I was hoping you'd take me to your party tonight," Lizzie said.

"Good thinking," Arno said, "Otherwise, who knows whether you would have gotten in. Wearing an outfit like that and all."

Lizzie giggled at that and slapped Arno's thigh in mock protest. She told the driver to take the long way to West 20th Street, and then she pressed into Arno and started kissing him breathily on the mouth. He put his hand on her stomach. He'd discovered that he really liked doing this—it was taught as a drum. He could tell she was totally excited about the special night with the four of them and was just being a little coy. Clearly, he was irresistible.

Arno listened to the rain falling on the roof of the car and decided that whatever was going to happen, he deserved it.

*

They arrived late, and Arno was unsurprised to see that the place was packed. Lizzie was hanging languidly from his arm. A cheer went up through the crowd when the people caught their first glimpse of Arno, and he waved at them dutifully before he and Lizzie headed over to the V.I.P. area.

Rob had actually done a good job picking out the space. It was huge, and it had big factory-style windows looking out on West 20th street, but it kind of looked like an apartment, too—smaller rooms had been built out at the back, and there were swinging doors, through which he could see a kitchenlike space, that looked like they had been salvaged from a painter's studio. The loft was in the right neighborhood, and it looked just arty enough.

Everyone he knew, sort of knew, or had passed on the street since he'd agreed to sign on with the whole party idea had wanted to know all about it. He was satisfied to see that they had all come, and then some.

Danny Abraham was there.

The bassist from the Backseat Rockstars was there.

Literally hundreds of people he didn't know were there. There were also a lot of people who looked older, like his parents' age, but everyone seemed to be drinking and dancing and having a good time.

Billy the DJ was there, too, DJ-ing for him,

apparently for free, even though he usually charged thousands of dollars a night.

Arno sat in the banquette, basking in all the adoration in the room. Lizzie was leaning against him, her white fur jacket slipping off her shoulders, and her bra straps with them.

He felt like the king of the world.

Rob came pushing through the crowd to get to them. He had a grin on his face that was so big and permanent he looked like the Joker.

"Terrible good news," he shouted over The Libertines, which DJ Billy was now blasting through the speakers. "We've already admitted four hundred people, and there's a line around the door!"

"That's great, man. Sweet party," Arno said. He was trying to appear blasé, but he couldn't help but smile a little bit, too.

Rob was nodding excitedly to himself. "And the monies! I—I mean me—I mean *we* have made so much of the monies tonight." A few bills fell out of his pockets, which he picked back up. He quickly added: "Which means we break even, of course."

Arno and Rob nodded to each other, and looked out at the great sea of coolness before them. Lizzie burped, and asked for another glass of champagne.

Out of the corner of his eye, Arno saw Jonathan with Flan and a bunch of her friends. Even with the loudness of the music, and the density of the crowd, he could feel the bitterness of Jonathan's stare.

David had arrived at Arno's big Saturday night party way too early, and by one in the morning, when the thing had really gotten going, he was feeling pretty tired and not too into it anymore.

His big plan had been to get there, avoid Rob, find Modigliani, and take her away with him. If she had been at the MoMA party, surely she would be at this thing, too. And if he could arrange it, he was going to straighten things out with Jonathan. The first part of the plan had been easy. Rob had been running around maniacally all afternoon, barking orders at the servers he'd hired, the security, the beer delivery person, and whoever else would listen. But many hours of the party had now passed without a sighting of the girl with the deep voice and the mole on her back.

All of his friends were acting like freaks, too. Except Patch maybe, who, true to form, was nowhere to be seen.

Jonathan wasn't making the make-up part of David's

plan easy, either. He had been standing in a little huddle with Flan and her girlfriends all night, pointedly ignoring David. Eventually the girls started dancing and hanging out with other people, but it looked like poor Flan was stuck with Jonathan, either sulking against the wall or making rounds to talk to other guys from Gissing.

Arno seemed to have rotated the It Girl on his arm, once again. It looked like Lizzie was the one scoring points in their little competition tonight. David decided he should definitely avoid that whole scene.

David couldn't help but notice that Sadie, the girl that Arno had at one point pushed him to hook up with, was gone, too. Her absence hadn't really made a dent, though. It Girls with whitish blond hair and artificial tans were everywhere. They seemed to be multiplying.

And just when David thought the night couldn't get worse, he caught his first glimpse of Mickey. And Mickey was naked.

David pushed through the crowd, and said "What's up?" to Mickey.

"Hey, man!" Mickey said. At least one of his friends was glad to see him. He felt kind of weird when Mickey gave him a naked hug, but he realized that he should probably just be glad that anyone wanted to hug him at all. "What's going on?"

"Oh, you know," David said. "Partying, I guess. But, um—you aren't wearing any clothes. You knew that, right?"

Mickey laughed like that was the funniest thing he had ever heard. Actually, he looked more bleary-eyed and crazed than usual. "Anyway," he said when he'd managed to stop laughing, "you're coming to the Fresh event, right?"

David was momentarily confused by Mickey's total nonchalance about the nudity thing, and said, "Yeah, I'll totally be there."

"Good man. It's been too long," Mickey said.

"Seriously," David said, "why are you naked?"

"Listen, if I want anyone to go to the Fresh event, I'm going to have to show them that it's okay. Bodies are beautiful. We can all be comfortable in the buff. It's like an advertisement."

"Are you okay?" David said instinctively.

"Shit, man!" Mickey was yelling now. "Never been better! Now I'm off to sell my body! I mean, my art!" Mickey headed into the crowd, calling back over his shoulder, "I'll call you with the details."

To David's surprise, a clump of girls standing nearby began responding to Mickey's naked event idea with huge enthusiasm. They all seemed to be giving him their numbers and asking if they were definitely in. He overheard one of them say, "Yeah, he's part of the Hottest Private School Boy's inner circle. I mean, there's no way it won't be hot. Arno's totally going to be there."

David moved away from them and over to where Jonathan and Flan were standing. Jonathan loved parties, David told himself, so perhaps he would be in a good enough mood that he would stop acting like a freak.

But as soon as he opened his mouth to say hello, he realized this was not the case.

"David," Jonathan said. "You really don't get it, do you? Everyone just likes you because you're friends with Arno. Nobody wants to hang out with you alone. Now would you get lost before you ruin my cred, too?"

David hung his head and turned to go. As he walked away, he thought he heard Flan say, "Why did you say that, Jonathan? It was so *mean*. . . ."

David thought he might actually cry. He desperately needed to leave this scene. He pushed through the girls writhing on the dance floor toward the door. On the way he saw Mimi, who hadn't disappeared after all. She was hanging on that Danny Abraham guy's arm now. After tonight, David wasn't going to be disgusted by anything ever again. If he could just leave this party right now, he was going to transform himself into a very hard kind of person who never let things get to him.

The coat check girl seemed to have abandoned her post, so he went into the little room right before the stairs to see what had become of his throwback Celtics warmup.

There was no coat check girl in there either, but there were four guys in police uniforms. Rob was there, too. And so was Jonathan's mom.

David was shocked. For a moment, he was happily convinced that this was all a weird dream.

"What I don't understand, Rob," Jonathan's mom was saying, "is how my Rolodex and ATM card ended up in the pocket of David's jacket. . . ."

"I am not understanding, either," Rob said. "Although it is all, how you say, coming together now. When I started arranging this party I am in a panic because the deposit on the loft is very gigantic. Then David say, *no worry Rob. I have ten thousand dollars, easy breezy*, and all of a sudden he have it. . . ."

David couldn't believe what he was hearing. He also couldn't believe how much thicker Rob's accent had gotten. Rob continued: "In my country, you see, we are not having much money at all, and so I think maybe ten thousand dollars, that's not all of that much in Nueva York. . . ."

"Well, it's not your fault, Rob. What we have to do is find David, and . . ."

"Dare he ees! Dare he ees!" Rob yelled. Everyone in the room turned to look at David. The guy who seemed to be the head cop moved toward him, and David flinched.

"Don't worry, young man," the head cop said. "We're just going to have to take you down to the station for some questioning."

"David," Jonathan's mother said, shaking her head.

"What are you doing here, Mrs. M?" David asked lamely. He had the unfortunate habit of acting guilty even when he wasn't. It had been this way since he was a little boy.

"Trying to get my money, and a little bit of my professional dignity, back in order," Jonathan's mother said coldly.

Just then, a couple fell through the door laughing. At first David thought it was one of the It Girls, but then he realized that it was only one of their many look-alikes at the party tonight. The dude appeared to be in his mid-thirties, and he looked like he was probably a professional during the week. His suit was a little rumpled now, though.

When the intruders saw the policeman, they started laughing even harder.

"Walter?" Jonathan's mother said, her mouth hanging open. "Walter Turbler from Merrill Lynch? What on God's green earth are you doing here?"

Walter stopped laughing and did his best to stand up straight. "Oh, hey. Um, your intern Rob called and invited me. Great party, by the way. Oh, and your portfolio is really looking good these days."

"My intern . . . Rob? You mean, David, don't you?"

"Yeah, Rob, David, whatever, something like that. Whoever it was said you were having a party here tonight, and he was confirming the guest list. Oh, by the way, he didn't put me on that list. I'm over it, it's cool, but if I could get a receipt for the door charge and the drinks, that would be great."

"Excuse me?" Jonathan's mom said.

"Never mind," Walter said. "I'll call you. We should set up a meeting about some new investment opportunities coming up." He pulled the It Clone with him, and as she went she raised her champagne glass to the policeman. "Bub-bye, officers," she said.

"Hold it right there," the head officer said. "How old are you, young lady?"

"I'll be eighteen in two weeks," she said proudly.

"Seems like we have some underage drinking here," the officer said sternly.

David couldn't believe what was going on. The night was getting exponentially more surreal, and now it was like he was in a cop movie. He was reminded that it was all very much *not* a movie, however, when the head cop pointed at him, and said, "Looks like you've been up to a heap of no good. Stealing, throwing parties, enabling underage drinking. Benson, cuff 'im."

David felt the cold hard metal around his wrists. Nope, not a dream or a movie. Then the officer started pulling him toward the door. He looked at Jonathan's mother for comfort, but she just shook her head and put her arm around Rob and squeezed him.

"David, you just didn't seem like the type," she said. "Not in my wildest dreams did I think you could throw a party like this. I mean, this is all utterly beneath contempt, but at the same time it's . . . very, well, it's very impressive."

Rob pulled away from her when she said that, looking like he was ready to throw a tremendous fit. "But he didn't do it!" Rob shrieked. "This was *my* party! I made the arrangements! I invited the cute underage girls! I stole the Rolodex and spent ten hours calling all of the professional contacts and telling them I would put them on the list so that they would come, when really only the celebrity people are on the list! David could never pull this off! It was me, all me!"

David felt the cuffs being taken off. He couldn't believe Rob would rather get arrested than not get credit for the party. The officer continued, "Benson, escort this woman home. Rodriguez, take this Rob character down to the station. I want you to get him to tell you everything." He turned to David. "Young man, you're free to go. But in the future, choose your friends more wisely."

Then he turned to the remaining officer and said, "Olenick, let's shut this party down."

i can't believe people are
having fun at this thing

"It just never fails to amaze me how sheeplike people can be," I said. I took a sip of my beer. It was one in a long line of beers.

"Tell me about it," Flan said.

"I mean, *New York* magazine says Arno Wildenburger is the Hottest Private School Boy, and all these people just believe it. Doesn't that make you a little bit sad? None of these people will ever have this Saturday night of their lives back. They'll have wasted it on Arno, and now it's almost over," I said.

"I know how they feel," Flan said.

"I mean, look, they even think David is cool," I went on, slurring slightly. I actually hadn't seen David in a while, but I could still quote most of the adoring magazine article, and the parts about David were especially drooltastic. At least he hadn't made a move on my girl yet. "And it's made him such an egomaniac he thinks he can get you back."

"What do you mean *back*?" Flan said hotly. Too bad for me, I was beyond listening to anyone else right then.

"I mean, only a huge media conspiracy could make all these people think Arno is cooler than I am, right? And David . . . Christ."

I didn't really think there was a media conspiracy at work here, but I did still, for that moment in time, think I was cooler than Arno. We were standing against the wall at his mega-event, which was, I had to admit, a pretty good party. But it mostly just reminded me how people are just magnets for "celebrity."

"Hey, what happened to your friends?" I asked.

"Um, I think you bored them to death," Flan said. "Thanks to you, all my friends are dead."

"What's that supposed to mean?" I asked. When you're in a relationship, there are just going to be a lot of little disagreements, and I was getting calmer and more grown up about handling them. But when I turned to look at Flan, I realized that this was not going to be your average tiff. The Balenciaga sack dress made her look a little childlike, especially with her hands on her hips as they were.

It might have made me laugh, if it hadn't made me feel so sad.

"Shut up, shut up, shut up!" she yelled loud enough that me and all the people near us could hear her above the music. "The one night—the one night!—we hang out with my friends you act like an egomaniac and talk about *you* the whole night! Well guess what, Jonathan? It's not always about you!"

Flan was really yelling now. And the thing was, she was right. All I'd talked about for the last week was me and how devastating this whole HPSB thing had been. To me. Even I was sick of . . . me.

It was like the whole room felt my shame. Suddenly, the music shut off, and the lights went up, like everybody had stopped talking.

And Flan wasn't done:

"You can be such a stupid idiot sometimes! I mean, whatever gave you the idea that you were so hot in the first place!"

I should have known that all the hubbub in the room had nothing to do with me. The lights had actually gone on, the music had actually gone off, and not because of me. There were actual policemen on the other side of the room yelling about how they were shutting this party down. But Flan kept on yelling. She was yelling so loud that everyone, including the police officers, stopped what they were doing and listened to her.

"You think you're soooo cool, right? You think you're cool enough to be named the Hottest Private School Boy, that Arno somehow robbed you of your birthright. Well, I got news for you, buddy, you aren't that hot, and Arno isn't, either. They didn't even want him to be HPSB. They wanted my brother, but you know what? He didn't call them back. He didn't want it. And you know why? Because he didn't need it. If you were really cool, Jonathan, you wouldn't be so anxious to tell everyone all the time. If you were really cool, you wouldn't be so insecure that you needed a magazine to tell you so."

Flan stared at me, her big eyes all full of anger instead of that usual sweetness. Her chest was nearly heaving with all that pent-up irritation.

I was floored, and as you might imagine, I had nothing at all to say.

The police officers did, though, and they said it through a bullhorn: "All right kids, party's over!"

And then everyone started rushing for the door.

something's all wrong with arno's star

Arno had been planning to start going to classes again that week, but when he woke up Monday morning he knew today wasn't going to be the day. He'd gotten pretty blitzed Saturday night, and after his party had been broken up, he'd gone somewhere else and gotten even drunker (it was all a little fuzzy, and he was trying not to think too hard about where he'd gone or whom he'd been with). All he'd really been able to do on Sunday was wake up in the afternoon, eat something, watch something on TV, not think, and go back to bed.

He still felt like shit now.

He made himself get out of bed, guzzle water, and do a couple reps of push-ups and crunches. That made him feel more awake, so he went into the bathroom to clean up. The sleep had done him well, it seemed—he still had a camera-worthy face. But today was definitely going to have to be a more healthy kind of day—he thought he'd maybe call Lizzie and see if she wanted to go get some green tea at Teany's on Rivington, take a long walk through Chinatown, catch a movie, and eat dinner at Angelica's Kitchen.

He wondered briefly if there was something he was supposed to do tonight—he felt like there was—but he couldn't for the life of him think what it might be.

It took him another fifteen minutes to find his phone, which was stuffed into the toe of his Nike Pigeons, for some reason.

He found her number in his contact list, and dialed it. Weirdly, after ringing twice, an automated message came on and told him that the number had been disconnected. Arno couldn't for the life of him think of a reason that a girl like Lizzie would have her phone disconnected. Then he remembered something about programming her number into his phone on the way to the party, because he hadn't had it before—maybe he just programmed it in wrong? They'd already started drinking, after all.

He called Mimi to try and get the number. This felt a little bit wrong, but what could he do? He was Arno fucking Wildenburger. She'd get over it.

But the same automated message came on when he dialed Mimi. Now, that was weird. But Arno had practically forgotten it already. He'd go out and get the tea, and probably Mimi and Lizzie would *both* call him within the hour. For a minute, he tried to think how he'd deal with that if it got messy, but it gave him a headache, and he had to stop.

Outside it was beautiful again—the rain had cleared the air, and as he strode down his town-house-lined Chelsea street, he started feeling healthier already. When he got to Eighth Avenue, he turned and started heading south.

There was something strange going on that Arno couldn't quite figure out. He thought about this all the way to 14th Street without a breakthrough. He was walking fast and distractedly, mulling it over, when he caught his toe on something large and lumpy and went flying forward. "Shit!" he yelled, twisting his head to see that the large and lumpy object bore his own image. He was going down fast, adrenaline coursing through his body, and at the last possible moment he grasped a parking meter and managed to swing himself upward.

Tripping in public was just not hot, he decided.

Arno jerked around and took a look at the object that had tripped him. It was the Hottest Private School Boy issue, lots of them, wrapped up and put at the curb to be recycled. They hadn't escaped the rain, though—there were muddy streaks and watermarks all over them. Arno realized, with a twinge of sadness, that they must have been out all night.

Then he realized what was weird about today. The

thing was that people weren't looking at him—at least, not the way they usually did. He wasn't feeling the warm caress of passing eyes, the soft murmurs of appreciation that had followed him around for the last week. That made him feel even more sad.

The sadness followed him as he continued on his way to the tea shop, and soon enough, the sadness turned into memory. The events of Saturday night started coming back to him. He shrugged his shoulders, trying to shake off the bad feeling, but it wouldn't go away. It was all coming back now: There was Lizzie in the towncar. There was Jonathan, giving him that nasty look. There were the drinks, lots of them. More Lizzie. Policemen. And then there was little Flan Flood, yelling at Jonathan in front of everyone about how uncool he was for wanting to be Hottest Private School Boy. Then she said something about how it was Patch who was supposed to be the HPSB. Not Arno.

Arno stopped walking, right in the middle of the sidewalk. There was more, but Arno made a strict rule with himself not to remember anything more from last Saturday. He decided that he couldn't handle the public right then, and hailed a cab that took him right back home.

There were three white cards sitting on the steps of his parents' brownstone. They were Tiffany engraved invitations, one for Mimi, one for Lizzie, and one for Sadie. The return address was his own. He had forgotten until that moment about the private party that night, and the invitations he had told Rob to send out. Each one was stamped with a big red, RETURN TO SENDER, and was still attached to a dozen wilted roses.

If there had been a convenient wall to punch, Arno Wildenburger would have punched it right then. All he could do was collect the invitations and put them right into the trash, where no one could see them.

When Monday morning rolled around again, I knew that one of the worst weeks of my life was over. But I didn't have that nice warm feeling called closure, either.

For one thing, I hadn't talked to Flan since the big blow-up Saturday night. We'd said good-bye kind of tensely, and then she and her crew all crammed into one cab and drove home. And while the HPSB issue, around which my life and ego had been revolving like toy planets in a fake universe for the last seven days, had been revealed as kind of a sham anyway—and Arno's status with it—I had been humiliated in a pretty public way.

Oh, and there were some pretty weird messages in my voicemail from my mom, too, which I hadn't had the strength to return.

It was enough to make that whole getting-out-of-bed thing even more of a challenge than usual.

When I walked into the kitchen, my mom was

sitting there drinking a cup of tea. She didn't look particularly mad at me, which was good, because I could just as soon do without a lecture on my late-night ways, or my limited ability to return stressful phone calls. Maria Callas was playing faintly in the background. Sometimes I think my mom has a little bit of a Maria Callas thing going on; she has very dramatic eyes.

"Good morning, darling," she said. "Would you like some tea?"

I sat down at the long, industrial-looking table that Mom keeps in the kitchen. It looks like you could do gourmet cooking or advanced chemistry on it, and believe me, nothing like that has ever happened in our apartment. She poured me a cup of steaming Irish Breakfast from a teakettle full of actual leaves.

"What's up, Mom?" I said, because clearly something was.

"Well, they're going to have to deport your friend Rob," she said, very carefully, like this news might wound me. "I know this might come as a blow to you, darling—we all thought he was doing so well. But I'm afraid the party he threw for Arno turned into rather a disaster—"

"Tell me about it."

"Yes, it seems he fancied himself something of a party promoter. Well, I spent all day with the police yesterday sorting this out, so I might as well tell you. But I wouldn't spread it around. Rob stole my ATM card and my Rolodex, and he took out quite a bit of money to finance his schemes of nightlife glory. He also called nearly all of my professional contacts and invited them to the party. It seems nearly everyone who came was assured they would be on the list, when in fact very few people were. Only the bold-faced names, it seems. All the money has been returned, thankfully—Rob's little event brought in quite enough to pay back what he stole from me and then some."

"Oh," I said. "Then why is he being deported?"

"Well, he's not really being deported in the technical sense. But his mother and I have talked, and it seemed like the best thing to do. What with the serving alcohol to minors charges and all. She's quite nice, really, this Penelope Isquierdo person. . . ." When my mom said that last part, she instinctively balled up her hands into fists. My mom let out a little gasp of air, and released the fists. "You know, your friend Patch called me Friday morning and told me he wasn't sure that I should have Rob living in my home."

"Patch did that?" I said. I hadn't even been sure that Patch knew Rob lived in my apartment.

"Yes, he did. He must have picked up on something the rest of us missed." Mom shook her head, like she couldn't believe such a person had been under her roof.

"What are you going to do with the extra cash?" I asked.

"Well, there's a Homeless Outreach program that Rob apparently sabotaged. All of the people who were supposed to go to their benefit ended up at Rob's event, so some of the surplus profit will go to them." My mom sighed. "There are really so many distasteful things he did, I don't know how the damage will ever be repaired."

I nodded slowly, trying to take it all in. "Hey, aren't you supposed to be at yoga?"

"Well, I'm afraid the stress of yesterday made me take up smoking again. I smoked a whole pack with the officers, maybe more, and I'm not feeling very holistic this morning, if you know what I mean."

I nodded in agreement. I wasn't sure I'd felt holistic ever.

"Well, what do you say we go down to Les Deux Gamins and have a little brunch, darling, just you and me?"

What with the bizarreness of it all, I decided that a quiet little breakfast with Mom before returning to the real world of school and image maintenance and talking with people my own age was probably a good thing. Just so long as she didn't want to talk about Flan.

Patch dug his toes into the sand and looked out at the gray-green Pacific Ocean. It was colder than the Atlantic, and a little bit rougher. But he liked it that way. People had always joked that Patch was more of a West Coast type, anyway.

He was at Steamer Lane, the big surfer beach in Santa Cruz. It was late afternoon, and the waves were crowded with wet-suited dudes and a few girls. One of them was Greta. She was even better than he'd remembered. Greta had big red hair and soft pink skin, and, just as he'd remembered, she was quiet and brave and a lot of fun. She waved to him, and he picked up the board he'd borrowed from her dad and ran down to the water.

The saltwater splashed in his face as he lay down on the board and paddled out toward where Greta and a bunch of guys were waiting for the next bunch of good waves. But he was wearing a wetsuit, too, and he didn't feel the cold so much. When he got to where Greta was, she pushed the wet tangle of red hair back from her forehead, and gave him a kiss that was cold and delicious.

He didn't know any of the other guys out there—there were six of them or so—but from the couple of days that he'd spent with Greta, driving around Santa Cruz, going to barbecues and seeing bands, it seemed like she knew everybody.

The next wave came up, and Patch went for it.

Out of the corner of his eye, he thought he saw a dark, wet-suited figure. But then there was just the exhilaration of rising up onto the board and riding the wave through the sea spray and biting air. He rode it almost back to the sand and then fell back into the ocean.

When he stood up, he saw three big dudes standing over him. They all had buzz cuts and fading tattoos of Jesus and Mary, or hearts and anchors. They didn't look particularly friendly, either.

"Hey, man," one of the guys said, "you dropped in on Flea." He had a big photorealistic tat of a smiling baby on his stomach, which was pretty muscled. His teeth were rotting, too.

Patch didn't know which guy Flea was, so he didn't say sorry right away.

"You from the college?" one of the other guys said.

"No," Patch said. "I'm from New York. I'm with Greta."

"What are you doing with Greta?" the smallest guy, who did look a little flea-like, said.

Patch smiled. "See, I used to think there wasn't anything that I really needed, you know? Anyone I wanted . . ." The guys were nodding. "But then I realized that I felt that way about Greta. And so I had to come from New York to get her. So here I am."

Greta smiled.

"Dude, that's kind of deep," Flea said.

A few hours later, they were all drinking beers around a bonfire and watching the sunset. Flea and his two friends had gotten a little sauced, and they started racing each other up and down the beach. Patch took the opportunity to run his fingers through Greta's hair, near the nape of her neck, and bring her face to his.

They kissed for a few minutes, and then Patch leaned back in the sand and said, "I wish I didn't have to go back."

Greta leaned back on her elbows and murmured in agreement. She had peeled her wetsuit down to her waist, and she was wearing a turquoise bikini on top. "Why do you have to?" she asked.

Patch thought about that for a minute. "School, I guess?"

Greta rolled over on her side, and bit her lip. "Maybe I could come with you?" she said.

"Don't you have school?" Patch said. Who was this pragmatic person speaking through him?

"Yeah, but I have spring break all this week. Maybe I could spend it in New York with you," she said.

Patch had to laugh a little bit at himself. He must have a spring break too, but he had no idea when it was. He'd probably missed it entirely, hanging around downtown, skateboarding, not even realizing that he wasn't cutting class.

"I mean, if that's too much too fast . . . I mean, we are just in high school, and long distance never works. Everybody knows that. I didn't mean to . . ." Greta trailed off, and started fidgeting with the dead skin around a sunburn on her shoulder.

Patch pushed himself up by the elbows, and gently hooked a finger at the waistband of her wetsuit. "Hey, Greta, I really, truly *want* you to come to New York with me."

David was taking a break from basketball practice when his phone rang for the first time since Saturday night. It took four rings to convince him that it was, in fact, his phone. He stared at it, and came to terms with the fact that it wasn't the Modigliani calling him.

He knew this because it was Rob's name flashing in his caller ID.

More out of instinct than anything else, he picked up. "Hi, Rob," he said guardedly.

"Daveed, my brother!"

"Um, yeah?"

"Well, I am calling to say good-bye. New York wasn't ready for me, you see!"

"Guess not." David was liking the way he sounded when he spoke in terse, two word sentences. It felt tough.

"They no getting my jokes, either," Rob was laughing, but it was the desperate laugh of a very sick person.

"How so?" David stood up and started to stretch. He

plucked open the sports top of his Gatorade bottle with his teeth.

"Oh, you know, the whole thingie with the police, and my whole joke telling them you had stolen the monies from Jonathan's mother instead of me. And, calling all of her special friends with power and influence. So funny, I am thinking! But they don't think that. But I am sorry I tell a joke like that that the world not understand. Do you forgive me, David?"

"Sure, Rob," David said. "I forgive you."

"Anyway, Mummie is sending me to a boarding school in England. So cold and boring there. No parties to throw. But no fear, David, I will be back."

"That's great," David said flatly. His teammates were starting practice back up again, and there was a lot of yelling and shouting in the gym.

Rob was still blubbering about how sorry he was, and how much he loved David and Arno as brothers. David was so astounded by the bullshit level here that he just kept on listening.

"Rob—what?" David yelled, as though he was going into a tunnel. "You're breaking up. I can't hear you." Rob continued to speak, but David just kept shouting like he couldn't hear him. "Okay, I'm hanging up now. If you can hear me, call later."

David tossed the phone back in his gym bag, and to

his total shock it started ringing again immediately. He picked it up, fully intending to send Rob's call straight to voicemail. But it wasn't Rob calling. It was Mickey.

"Hey, man," he said.

"David, what's the latest?" David didn't really know where to begin. Luckily, Mickey kept right on talking. "So, I know things got sort of crazy Saturday night."

"Tell me about it."

"But the good news is, when I got the citation from the cops, there were some tabloid people hanging around."

"You got a citation?"

"Yup, public nudity. But more importantly, I got in the *Post*, dude!"

"The *New York Post*?" David asked idiotically.

"Totally. And the caption mentioned how I was advertising the naked restaurant event at Fresh. Isn't that awesome? Anyway, I just wanted to give you the info."

"For the naked thing?"

"Yeah, remember you told me you were in on it Saturday night. Do *not* punk out on me, man."

David paused and looked at all his teammates running around on the court. They were all pretty straight. He wondered what they would think of him taking part in a nude group photo shoot.

"Yo, Grobart, you want to get in on this game or what?" The coach yelled irritably.

"Yeah, I'm in," David yelled back at his coach.

"Great," Mickey said. "So, I'll see you at around six, this Thursday at Fresh, right?"

"Grobart, now is not the time to plan your social calendar!" Coach yelled. Some of his teammates laughed. David had been catching a lot of flack for the way that magazine had portrayed him as a loafing party dude.

"One second!" he yelled back. "Hey, Mickey, do you maybe want to hang out before then? It's been a long time."

"Okay," Mickey said. "But I'm going to have to be making a lot of phone calls. This naked thing has taken over my life."

"It's cool," David said.

"Okay, meet me at Passerby at eight, and we'll have a beer."

"Sweet."

This made David so happy, he really didn't even care that all his teammates were laughing and calling him a girl and asking if he'd take them with him when he got his next manicure.

"So what's been going on, Mickey?" David asked, when they were comfortably settled into the corner of Passerby. It was Mickey's second-favorite bar, both because it had a disco floor (and Mickey liked all things loud and unnecessary), and because the owner was a crazy British gallery owner who could out-drink Mickey *and* who treated him like art world royalty.

"Mostly planning the naked restaurant thing," Mickey said. "It's really taking off. It's like everybody wants to know about it. It's going to be huge."

"That's great," David said. Although he was feeling pretty wary of all things "huge," he instinctively wondered if Modigliani might be there. "You seem really busy."

"Yeah, I'm trying. Can I tell you something, dude?" David nodded.

"I went to Meow Mix—you know that lesbian bar way east on Houston—to try and get some lesbians in on the naked restaurant event. And Philippa was there. Making out with another girl."

"Whoa," David said. Somehow, he had assumed that he would be the first one of his crew to face the coming out of a girlfriend or recent ex-girlfriend. This was a pleasant surprise, but he tried to make sure that that didn't show in his face.

"Yeah, I guess it's really over between us this time. Philippa likes girls."

"Weird that she was with a guy like you all this time," David said. He hoped that sounded like a compliment.

"Mmm," Mickey said. "Good point."

"Yeah," David said, at the same time as Mickey's phone rang.

"Whassup," Mickey said into the phone. "Oh, hey Arno. . . . Yeah man, of course you're still invited to Fresh. . . . Just hanging with David . . . Passerby—of course you can come. . . ."

Mickey and David looked up, and to their surprise, Arno was standing, waiflike, in the window.

i start picking up the pieces

It had sort of gotten around that something really bad had happened to Mickey in the Philippa department, and so on Tuesday afternoon, when he called and asked for my help, I figured I should probably say yes.

I went over to his house, which is kind of near Patch's on Perry Street. His dad's sculpture studio is there, too. In fact, when I rang the doorbell, it was none other than Ricardo Pardo who greeted me at the door. His signature shock of graying hair rose up from his forehead and fell to somewhere around his chin, and he was wearing denim overalls without a shirt underneath.

"Good, Jonathan," he said gruffly when he saw me.

"Hey, Mr. Pardo," I said meekly. I still feel a little weird around Mickey's dad, because last winter this thing came out about how my dad stole a bunch of money from Mickey's dad and all my friends' parents, back in the eighties. He didn't seem to be thinking about that now, though.

"Talk some sense into Mickey, will you?" he said as I followed him through the big, spare first floor of their house. "All he can talk about is his art project. Tell him he doesn't want to be an artist. Art's a racket, and he'll just end up enslaved to other people's perceptions of him."

This conversation seemed a little inappropriate to me, given our parent/teenager status, but I tried to nod in agreement as much as possible.

"Good," Mr. Pardo said when we got near Mickey's room. He seemed to think that took care of things. "Stay for dinner if you want."

I went into Mickey's room, which was the usual mess of clothes and CDs. Mickey was lying on his bed with his hands behind his head and his elbows in the air, chatting into the headset of his cell phone.

"Sweet, thanks Sandra," Mickey was saying. "I'm so glad you want to do it. I'm going to put you down for a four-top, but you can fit five. You plus four, right? Awesome. See you there."

Mickey jumped up from the bed and tackled me.

"Hey, man, I missed you, too," I said when he stood up.

"Yup," Mickey said, grinning. "Thanks for coming over, man. I have, like, eighty confirmation calls to make for the Fresh project Thursday night, and I was sort of hoping you could do it with me."

"Totally," I said. I love making phone calls. I still didn't know all the Philippa details, but I thought that if Mickey was hurting, then a distraction was probably good. I couldn't help but add, "Although I wish you'd called me back, at least once, last week."

"I know," Mickey said. "I was really distracted by shit with Philippa. I think it's really over between us, you know?"

"I know," I said.

Then we hustled through the list. It was actually a pretty impressive roster of people, not boldfaced names or anything, but cool kids that we knew from being around so long. And everyone I talked to sounded really excited. I still didn't completely believe he could pull it off, but he certainly had taken this whole thing further than I thought he would.

When I looked at the seating chart, I noticed that the table next to us was populated by girls from Florence, including Mimi Rathbone and her sidekicks. I had seen Mimi making out with Danny

Abraham on Saturday, and I wasn't sure Arno would want to be sitting near her. But I decided Mickey probably didn't need more shit to worry about, and didn't say anything.

When we were done, Mickey said, "Thanks, dude. Don't know how I could have done that without you. Don't know how we did anything without you, actually."

I didn't know quite how to respond to that, but it made me feel like some of my dignity might be recovered. "You wanna go get a beer or something?"

"Nah, I gotta keep a low profile, make sure I don't mess this thing up. But I set up a table for you, Arno, Patch, and David. And we should all hang out afterward. I had a beer with David yesterday, and Arno showed up pretty messed-looking. I think it would be pretty important, you feel me?"

"Yeah," I said, and I did.

"And that Rob guy? We talked about that, too. He was bad news."

"Yeah," I said, but I hadn't even told them the worst of it. "Anyway, I guess I better get going. But I'll see you tomorrow?"

"You know it." Mickey and I knocked our fists

together lightly and said bye. As I headed out the door, he called out, "Oh, should I put Flan at your table?"

I was once again flushed with panic. Moral quandary: Can you take your fourteen-year-old girlfriend to participate in an event where you and all your closest guy friends are going to be wearing absolutely nothing? Does the situation change if your last interaction was a big blow-up fight? And what if she was very right about you and your insecurity, and underneath it all, you're afraid your guys might all look better naked than you?

**but i do have to expose myself
sometimes. emotionally speaking**

After I left Mickey's, I wandered down Perry Street in the Manhattan night. It was misty and pungent, and you could really sense that a whole lot of people were living big, bright lives all around you. I didn't really know where any of this—Flan, my crew, the Rob fallout—was going, and for once that really didn't bother me.

I went to the Floods' and knocked on the door. A few minutes later, Flan poked her head out. When she saw me, she smiled sadly and came out and put her arms around my waist. We kind of swayed like that for a minute, not feeling the need to say anything. Flan was wearing flip-flops and a strapless cotton dress that looked like it was made from terry cloth. After we did our slow, funny little dance, we sat down on her stoop.

"I've been thinking a lot about Saturday night," she said.

"Yeah, me too."

"And I'm really sorry I made such a fuss in front of so many people."

"I'm not mad about that. You were right, I was being a gigantic narcissist. I mean, I was just being freakishly insecure. And I'm sorry." We were both talking really slowly, like we knew where this was headed but neither of us was quite ready to go there. The night was such a warm, get-crazy kind of night, too, and that made the sad talk all the more poignant.

Flan puffed out her cheeks, so that she looked kind of like the cutest monkey ever. Saddest *and* cutest.

"We have to break up, Jonathan," she said, blowing the air out of her mouth. She sounded very calm, like a person far older than she actually was. I had kind of been expecting that, but that doesn't mean it felt good. "It's not that I don't like you, because I really like you. But you know what? Our lives are really different right now."

"Like, how?" I said. I wasn't really sure why I was arguing this—she was obviously right. "I like going to parties, you like going to parties. We both like French films and ice cream. We both have great friends."

"I know, but . . ." Flan threw her arms up in exasperation with herself this time. I think. Her eyes were glistening a little bit, too; at least, I think they were. "It's just that, when I'm with you, everything has to be so jaded all the time. I know it's kind of dumb, but I just want to do fun, silly stuff with my friends, and not be so worried about looking cool all the time."

"I'm totally over being cool," I said defensively.

"You are not, and besides, that's not what I mean. You've done all the things I want to do now, and I just want to do it and be excited about it and not be so knowing all the time. I don't want to miss the feeling of doing something for the first time, just because I'm with some cool older guy."

"Yeah . . . ," I said, because there really isn't any way to argue with a speech like that.

"I know that's dorky, but . . ."

"That's not dorky," I said, even though it hurt me to say so. "That actually makes a lot of sense. You should have fun, and be with your friends. They adore you, you know."

"I know."

"There's never been anything between you and David, has there?"

"No. In fact, I think Rob was maybe just trying to make you think there was."

"Oh." Rob was turning out to be pretty convenient, actually. I wondered what else I could blame on him. I picked Flan's hand up and said, "I'm always going to think you're pretty special."

"Yeah, you, too," she said, and smiled the sad, calm smile. I couldn't believe that after all this time I was going to lose Flan, and my insides felt heavy.

We stood up and kissed—a long, slow good-bye kind of kiss—on the stoop, and then I jumped down to the street and waved and turned toward home. My lungs got all full of that warm city air, and as I walked and thought about it, suddenly this news didn't seem so crushing after all. There was still the city, after all, and my friends. I started to feel really light and open.

And, I should admit, it didn't hurt to know that I wouldn't be hanging out with Flan—and all of my closest friends—in the nude tomorrow night.

mickey has a thing or two
left to learn about girls

"Don't get me wrong, I understand being attracted to chicks and all," Mickey said. "What I don't get is why, if you're, like, gay and shit, you were with a dude like me all this time."

Philippa rolled her eyes at Mickey, but it was a loving kind of eye roll. It was the day they were supposed to have their afternoon therapy session, but since they'd broken up they didn't have to go anymore. Which they both thought was awesome. They'd decided to celebrate with tea and cookies at Doma, this café down the street from where they both lived.

"Maybe I was too much, like, I turned you off men?" he went on.

"That is *so* something a man would say," she laughed. "As though my liking a girl or not liking a girl could only be understood through my previous relationship with a man. Yeah, right. It's not like I wasn't attracted to you. And it's not like I wasn't your match, so don't pretend like I should have been going out with some girly man all this time. I just realized that I feel more myself with another girl. Does that make sense to you?"

"Not really. But I'm trying."

Philippa took a sip of her tea. "Are you doing okay?"

"Yeah!" Mickey said facetiously. "I mean, come on, it's going to take me a while to get over a girl like you. But I'll be all right. How 'bout you? You told your folks yet?"

"No," Philippa said, grinning. "But I can't wait. Can you imagine? They are going to be *so goddamn mad.*"

They both cracked up at that.

"Steam's gonna come out of your dad's ears!"

"I know!" Philippa cried, practically choking on her tea. "And can't you just picture my mom? She's going to sob."

"She's going to break down!" Mickey hooted. He calmed himself down somewhat and said, "You're not just doing this so that you can find bigger and better ways to make your parents suffer, are you?"

"No! Mickey, please believe me. I am a lesbian. Nothing to do with you. Okay?"

"Okay."

"Good. Now tell me, how's this nude thing going?"

Mickey shrugged. "I don't know if people are going

to go for it. It might just be me and the waitstaff, you know?"

"Well, I'll be there," Philippa said.

"Really?"

"You bet."

The day of the big nude art event, I decided I had to make that call. I sat down at my desk and looked out my window and dialed David's number.

He picked up after two rings. "Hey, man."

"Hey, David?" I said. "I just wanted to say I'm sorry. I've been a real dickhead."

"No you haven't . . . er, I mean, I've been out of touch, too."

"C'mon David, I don't mean out of touch. Every time we've seen each other over the last week I've been downright nasty," I said. This was surprisingly not that hard to say.

"Yeah, but I knew Rob was trying to make you jealous over me, and I really didn't try hard enough to stop it."

"David, would you shut up and let me apologize like a man?"

"Okay."

"I am really and truly sorry for all the mean

things I've said, and all the dumb ways I've acted over the week. I hope you still want to be friends with me." I pounded my fist on the windowsill when I was done.

"Yeah, man. I still want to be friends with you," David said.

"So, you wanna come over and have some beers before we go to this event of Mickey's?" I asked.

"Shit, is that tonight already? I guess I was sort of hoping it wouldn't come up so soon."

"Yes," I said, "it is tonight. And believe me, man, I hear you."

mickey wants to see what you've got under all that hot, restrictive clothing

"You brought a good crowd," Philippa said, leaning her elbow against Mickey's shoulder and surveying the room. Everyone was surprised and pleased by the chummy, platonic way in which Mickey and Philippa were already getting along.

"Crazy, right?" Mickey was still sort of incredulous that all these people had shown up. "Thanks for coming," he added.

"Wouldn't miss it. I better go find my group," Philippa said, pointing to a table of well-put-together, if slightly tough-looking, lesbians. Mickey waved at Sadie, who seemed to have found a new crew to run with, and she waved back.

There were a few hours yet before the dinner rush, but the staff of Fresh was already darting in between tables and refilling carafes of water anxiously. It was naked night, and none of them really knew what to expect.

But Mickey Pardo, who was standing at his post by the entrance, seemed to be looking at exactly what he'd expected. The spare room, with its shiny black bamboo floors and chrome-and-mirror walls, was filled with kids searching for their name cards, shouting hellos and blowing kisses. Mickey crossed his arms over his chest and grinned.

"Hello, beautiful people!" he called out. "Let's all take a seat, please."

At a table right and center of him, he saw David, Arno, and Jonathan taking their places. They'd come in together, and seemed to be getting along just fine. There was no Patch yet, though. David and Arno were dressed casually, but Jonathan was wearing the same camel suit he'd worn to the MoMA party. He looked pretty dressed up, and Mickey wondered briefly if he was going to have trouble taking the thing off. Mostly he was just glad Jonathan was there.

His assembled friends and acquaintances took their seats, giggling and talking as they did.

The manager of the restaurant came up to Mickey. His names was Yves, and he was nervously rubbing the round protrusion of his belly. "It's already six-thirty," he said.

"Yeah, I know," Mickey said. He didn't actually know, of course. Mickey almost never knew the exact time. But the fact that it was six-thirty didn't worry him.

"Well, you know the dinner people are coming soon," Yves said. "This thing doesn't seem to be moving along very fast. Nobody is naked yet."

"Yeah," Mickey said. "You're right." He thought about this for a moment, and then he called out to the assembled room, "Take yer clothes off!"

The room burst into excited laughter, but nobody moved to disrobe. Then they all went back to talking. Mickey looked at Yves, who looked distressed.

"It has to be kind of like a party, you know what I mean?" Mickey said.

Yves nodded. He motioned to the head waiter. A few minutes later, the waiters moved about the room pouring flutes of champagne and serving little dishes of cold black rice and radish appetizers. This seemed to make everybody happy.

"Great," Mickey bellowed to the crowd. "Now, show me what you got."

The crowd was still resisting his commands, so Mickey pulled off his shirt and dropped his camouflage pants to the ground. He did a little naked spin for the crowd, which cheered him. There were catcalls, especially from the lesbians.

Amidst the excitement that followed, a few people

stripped down to their underwear (Philippa and her friends were part of this advanced guard), but pretty soon the guys were just staring at the panty-clad girls, and all disrobing came to a halt.

Besides Mickey, the nakedest dude in there was David, who was a loyal-enough friend that he'd stripped down to his boxers in solidarity.

Mickey was beginning to think that Luc Vogel did actually have it rough. How did he do this, year after year? How was Mickey ever going to get all these people to take their clothes off?

"Can I just say that you look *amazing* in your undies?"

David instinctively distrusted this statement, and not only because it was the first time he'd heard it. He was an athlete, after all—he had the broad shoulders and long muscled legs of a guy who played basketball every day of his life—so he was going to hear something like that sooner or later. No, it was the sickeningly sweet voice of the speaker, sitting over to his right, that made him narrow his eyes.

"Thanks," he said, turning warily to see whom it was.

"Hey, David," Lizzie said, smiling. It certainly wasn't Modigliani, whom he'd been looking for all night. In fact, he had been so focused on looking for her that he had somehow not noticed when everyone else stopped taking their clothes off, and now he was the only guy in the room down to his boxers.

He could feel her looking at his crotch, and he was very relieved that he'd been paying enough attention not to go completely buck naked. "Oh, hi, Lizzie," he said grudgingly.

The It Girls had stripped down to their bras and jeans, and he could see that her breasts looked kind of swollen—abnormally spherical, almost. A girl he was pretty sure was Mimi ran her eyes up and down David's body approvingly. Who knew if it was really her, though—they still all looked really similar to him, and after several days sans It Girls, he could no longer tell them apart.

"Yo, Lizzie," Arno called from over his shoulder.

She looked over at Arno, and then quickly turned away.

"Lizzie, it's Arno," he continued. "I guess Monday didn't work out, huh? Sorry I haven't called, but I guess I programmed your number into my phone wrong."

"Uh . . . bummer. Remind me to give it to you before we leave," she called over her shoulder, before burying her face in Mimi's shoulder and bursting out in giggles.

David was pissed that they were laughing at his friend, and he was about to say something when he was distracted by a stray imperfection in the crew of plastic girls seated next to them. It was a large, dark mole at the narrowest part of a girl's back.

The Modigliani! She was right there! Sitting with the

It Girls, her dark hair twisted over her shoulder, and she seemed to be laughing. She had taken off her shirt and was now wearing a bra and super low-rise jeans. David stood up, and walked over so that he was standing right behind her.

"I've been looking for you everywhere," he said. She turned around very slowly, and all her blond friends looked with her. Their faces were full of admiration.

"I've been looking for you, too," she said. She was smiling a perfect, blindingly white smile.

The only thing David could think to say was "Sorry, I thought you were somebody else," but he couldn't even get that out. He was completely speechless, because it *was* her, but she didn't look anything like before. Now she was just so . . . bland.

"Do you like it?" she said. He could only assume that she was talking about the perfect ski jump that her once unique nose had been converted to. And he didn't have anything to say about that. "I got it done the day after we met, and I haven't been out until now because I was waiting for the swelling to go down. What do you think?"

David decided that she had definitely had more than just her nose done. She looked just like all the other girls at her table, except that she had brown hair, at least for now. David must have been stunned into honesty, because he said, "No, I don't think I do like it," out loud, and then he stumbled backward toward his table, knocking over a chair on his way.

"Hey, you okay, man?" Jonathan said. All his guys cracked up a little bit at his klutziness.

"All these girls think you're hot; don't fuck it up," Arno said, slapping David on the back.

But David was feeling all quiet and exhausted with disappointment, so he excused himself to go to the bathroom. He was trying to figure out which way the bathroom was when he heard someone calling his name. He turned and saw Sandra Anderson. She was sitting with a bunch of her friends at a table. And he discovered that he was disappointed that she was still wearing all her clothes.

"Did you have a good time at the party last week-end?" he said idiotically. Then he saw the look on Sandra's face, and remembered what Rob had said about her being "super uncool and a little ugly" and realized just *how* idiotic it was. "Hey, I'm sorry about Rob. He didn't act in a way I'd ever want a friend of mine to act."

"Yeah, that really sucked. Rob, I mean," she said.

"I know," David said.

"Well, it's good to see you, anyway."

"Yeah, um . . . can I get your number before we leave?" David said. He made a little gesture and said, "I don't have a pen on me, as you can see."

240

"Of course you can have my number," she said, smiling happily.

"Okay, don't forget, though."

"David, that's really not going to happen." Sandra winked at him, and David smiled to himself as he walked away.

When he made his way back to his table, he felt like he'd let go of something really heavy and self-destructive.

Mickey was still acting like a cheerleader at the front of the room, and Jonathan and Arno still seemed to be getting along fine. Jonathan hadn't said a single mean thing to him tonight.

"Is he going to be able to do it?" David asked as he sat down. Jonathan still had his suit on, and Arno was wearing jeans but no shirt.

"I don't know, man, this seems like a tough crowd," Arno said.

Just then, the door opened and a gust of warm night air blew over the nervous, giggling crowd.

I was starting to get worried for Mickey—he had been up there trying to get everyone to take their clothes off for almost an hour now. But then the front door of the restaurant opened, and in came Patch with that girl Greta right behind him.

Everyone got very quiet, and I heard Mimi Rathbone and her crew whispering about how he was the *real* Hottest Private School Boy. I also heard one of them saying, a little louder than was strictly speaking necessary, "But who's he with? She doesn't look like anybody, does she?"

Patch was still talking to Mickey. "Hey, I'm not late, am I?" he said.

"Naw, man, just getting started," Mickey said back. I wondered if Mickey would be weird about Greta, since after all, he had pursued her hardcore last winter. But then she gave him a very sisterly kiss on either cheek, and everything seemed okay. Mickey pointed them in our direction, and the whole restaurant watched as we loudly greeted our long-lost friend. Greta gave us each a kiss on the cheek, too.

Then Patch and Greta astounded us all by pulling their shirts over their heads, and pulling their jeans over their ankles. Neither of them had been wearing underwear, and they both looked tan and freckled naked.

They sat on the chairs in front of our table like it was the most natural thing in the world, and then Greta poured us each a glass of champagne, and said, "Cheers, guys. It's really good to see you."

And then we all clinked.

That did it, I guess, because to my utter amazement, everyone in the room started taking their clothes off right then. Patch and Greta just made being naked look so cool that everyone else became instantly comfortable with it. Arno stripped down to nothing, and then when David pulled his boxers down, he set off another whole round of whistles and appreciative murmuring.

Pretty soon, the whole room was a sea of bare skin and naked thighs and bellies. Mickey started taking pictures, and everyone posed for him and moved as he said. There was a lot of teasing and laughing, but everyone managed to hold still, more or less, when Mickey told them to.

I couldn't do it, though.

I just couldn't take my clothes off in front of all those people. I stayed right where I was, with my suit jacket on and my shirt buttoned up to the collar.

In my own defense, I'd like to say that the events of Saturday night had been enough public naked-ness for me for one week. And somehow the idea of being totally bare in front of your best people is a little frightening. But after some teasing and cajoling, everyone sort of forgot that I was wearing a suit. Maybe it was because it was beige, and I almost blended in.

Otherwise, everyone was extremely naked. There were so many exposed breasts that I didn't even really care about looking at them anymore. The whole thing had kind of turned into a party— even the waitstaff was drinking, and I'm pretty sure they started turning away people at the door, even the ones with dinner reservations. A blue-grass band had appeared out of nowhere and set up in the corner, and were now playing energeti-cally. In the buff.

Me and my guys were all getting along, too. It was almost like we hadn't just spent a lot of time alienated from and resenting each other. I'd apologized to Arno for being a dick, and he'd blown it off like it didn't matter at all. And then we'd actually hugged. Before he was naked, obviously. Then, when Mickey had taken enough pictures of the room, he came over to the table, and we all toasted to his success.

"Mickey, I think you might be a genius," Patch said.

"Nah," Mickey said. "I'm just crazier than all y'all put together."

"Can I take a picture of you?" Greta said. We all said yeah, and she took a digital camera out of her bag, and stepped away from us so that she could get the best shot. Then the flash went off several times. She laughed happily at the results. "They weren't lying. You guys really are pretty damn hot." Then she passed the camera around so we could see what we looked like.

There we were, four naked guys and me in my Duncan Quinn suit. And we *did* look cool. Not overly posed or hyped cool, just like a bunch of guys who knew who they were, whether they were totally revealing it or not. I had the feeling that we were all going to be okay with each other after tonight.

They kept Fresh closed to the usual dinner crowd, and most of the naked people stayed really late. It seemed like we had to talk to all of them, but as much as we could, we just talked to each other, filling each other in on where we had been and where we were headed next.

Don't miss *Hold On Tight*, the next Insiders book!

The guys have gotten way too notorious for the city. Did someone say road trip?

Jonathan visits his brother at college . . . will Ted out-cool him?

Mickey is taking his naked pictures on tour . . . what will he photograph next?!

Arno finds his first love . . . now he needs to figure out where she went.

Patch searches for the perfect college to reunite with Greta . . . but are they destined to be together?

David has an amazing new girlfriend . . . until she moves in with his family!

While you wait, check out the boys' latest on www.insidersbook.com.